DARK PLAGUE
SPECIAL EDITION

DARK PLAGUE
SPECIAL EDITION

C. M. Parsons

authorHOUSE®

AuthorHouse™
1663 Liberty Drive
Bloomington, IN 47403
www.authorhouse.com
Phone: 1-800-839-8640

Published by AuthorHouse 02/11/2013

ISBN: 978-1-4817-0404-5 (sc)
ISBN: 978-1-4817-0403-8 (e)

Library of Congress Control Number: 2013901917

TABLE OF CONTENTS

DARK PLAGUE: SPECIAL EDITION

We're outside of Earth as it rotates with satellites passing by, and as they pass by, we begin picking up communications of what seems to be news feed from around the world.

(NEWSWOMAN)
Are you telling us that the rumors of server side effects were over exaggerated?

(MAN)
I'm saying there are no side effects. We've been doing studies since 2001 with rates and the outlook has always been good.

(NEWSWOMAN)
Well the pictures say otherwise. Rat bodies showing signs of serious mutations. Looking almost, zombified. How do you . .

(MAN)
Look, I don't know where you're getting your materials or who's your source. What I am telling you is that the CDC has been watching over us for the past 20 years along with the Secretary of Defense because of the technology being used.

Scene changes to the UN with Secretary of Defense Ted Jelanski at the podium speaking to the leaders of other nations.

(JELANSKI)
I guarantee to all of you, we are not secretly building a weapon of mass destruction. Top officials of your nations have been monitoring us for almost a quarter of a century.

There's muttering among the crowd with disbelief.

(JELANSKI)
This was not only a sign of good faith between our people,
but insurance that this medical breakthrough happens, so
that the obesity in our nations is handled without us giving
up the things we love. Why not have our cake and eat it
too? With the final results and the CDC on board, Gene-tech
Industry will be shipping out millions of cases within weeks.

The scene changes to stores all over the world with trucks
pulling up and silver cases are being unloaded to the pharmacy
departments for sell. Hospitals are seeing huge numbers of
patients swarming through the doors not because sickness or
injuries, but of over weight people who wants what's being said
as a gift from heaven.

(FATHER)
Come on! Let us through! You people aren't even sick.

Officers already prepared for this starts coming in to force
the one massive line into single lines so that the man and his
sick daughter can get through. One of the nurses behind the
protective glass is carrying over a tray of the liquid cure
for those with prescriptions. She stumbles and drops one of the
tubes, which shatters on the floor, letting out the material.

(NURSE#1)
SHIT!

(OVERWEIGHT PATIENT)
That better not be mine!

(NURSE#2)
Don't worry. They're not active outside the body. Go ahead
and clean it up. I'm surprised you're even here as sick as
you are.

(NURSE#1)
Another day, another dollar.

The nurse picks up the shattered tube and cuts herself and
sucks on her bleeding finger as an ant crawls along the floor

and stops in front of the spill. A rolled up news paper comes down on it hard, leaving the smashed ant soaking lifeless.

(DOCTOR)
This place is supposed to be cleaned. Call Peter. Have him check this floor for vermin.

(NURSE#2)
Yes, doctor.

The nurse comes back with paper towels and a bottle full of some type of sanitizer. Unknown to her, the smashed ant was gone.

(PETER)
Hey, you guys have a clean up?

(NURSE#1)
No. We just need this floor checked for bugs.

(PETER)
No problem.

(NURSE#2)

Oh, can you take that can of trash with you?

(PETER)
Sure.

Peter takes the small bag of trash that had the rolled up newspaper partially covered in the metallic liquid out of the bin and ties it up tightly. Out the back door of the hospital comes Peter tossing the bag of trash into the dumpster. A cat is startled and jumps out.

(PETER)
Stupid cat.

The door closes and the cat comes out of hiding to jump back into the dumpster, scavenging for food. We get closer to the dumpster as we begin hearing a voice.

(ALEX)
We don't know how it started, where it started, or when. We just know that a single moment in time marked the beginning of a possible end for humanity.

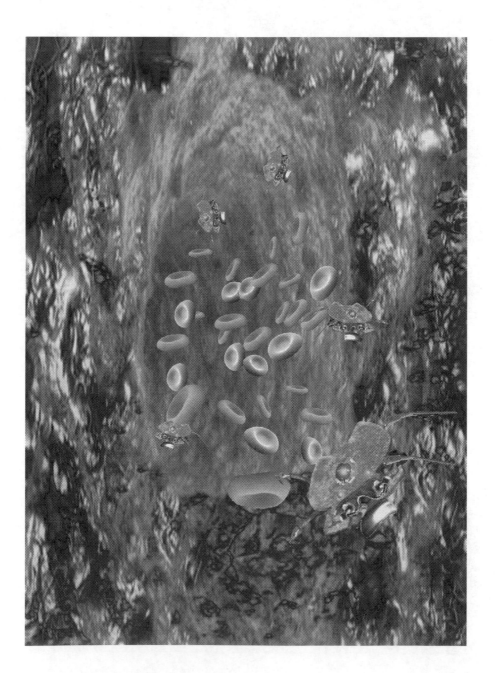

We're now journeying within the human body seeing organs and blood cells traveling throughout. There's a dark orchestral music playing. Now dark blobs with metallic spikes appear from below chasing after the blood cells and the music gets darker and faster. Incomes the white blood cells. Unsuccessful, the white blood cells are over taken and the tissue within the body continues to decay along with the organs. We continue to pass on to view a decaying heart and through the neck, finally up to eyes. We go through the eyes, panning outwards to see the face of a dead body with the title "Dark Plague" fading onto the screen with rain starting to come down.

SOUND OF LIGHTNING STRIKES . . .

Now going across the ocean, we see the sun setting in the distance with thick grey clouds continuing to form, indicating that a storm is on its way. Making its way through the still waters is an armored boat with a figure flickering switches up and down. He's turning dials with one hand and monitoring a compass with the other. The man cranks forward the throttle and speeds towards a small island barely visible in the far distance.

The boat is parked and the man wearing dark clothing drops a duffle bag to the ground. He then climbs down the ladder, picks up the bag and heads into the city. Everything goes black.

                    ALEX (voice over)
            Atlanta, code name: Sector 5.
            Or as I call it, hell on Earth.

Still frames of Black and White images of a city flashes before us as a van is seen passing a military checkpoint.

                    ALEX (voice over)
Two others and myself were sent in to confirm whether there were survivors as first indicated. It was a foolish idea. But like good little soldiers, we did as we were told.

Still framed images continues on. Gun-fire, screams, and monstrous roars can be heard. Alex and two other I.P. Agents can be seen fighting zombies and mutants with a few survivors from the city.

                    ALEX (voice over)
I didn't think any of us would of made it out alive. But as luck would have it, the three of us escaped with survivors and information that would bring down a mayor and his plans for world domination.

    Scene changes with us coming through the fog to view the abandoned streets of Charish Port with torched cars, tipped over fire trucks and ambulances covered in trash. But, strangely enough no bodies.

    Alex walks across the street by a broken bus. As if something huge tore it with its bare hands. You can see a sign on the side of a building. "Emergency Entrance." Alex looks up as he stands in front of a huge automatic door. The doors aren't working and the light breeze sends trash fluttering around the torched vehicles and an American flag above a barber shop waves towards the sky as if it was waving to the moon itself. Alex continues walking with a PDA in his hand.

                    ALEX (voice over)
Now I'm in a new type of hell. Ground zero of the plague. Not for more data, but for my kid brother. Who I was in contact with via internet a day ago.

    Alex enters through a broken window of the hospital as quietly as he could. Everything is trashed, with blood on the walls and a phone off the hook, still with power as we can hear a dial tone. Alex walks over and picks up the receiver to see if he can reach anyone. But as soon as he puts it to his ear, the phone goes out. He drops the receiver down and heads down the hallway. Coming to an elevator, Alex presses the buttons to get some sort of reaction. The elevator won't budge and the elevator on the other side has torn doors with the elevator missing.

   He sees a door that leads to stairs that goes to the upper levels of the hospital. As he opens the door, thick veins are covering the walls. A door opens on the 20th floor as Alex looks through to see a couple of rodents and a cat-like animal chewing apart a large body. His PDA shows that he's closer to the signal and that it leads to the office ahead.

Alex pulls out a small black ball that gives off a flash and everything nearby scatters away. Alex enters a doctor's office to see bullet holes on the walls and furniture flipped upside down. He turns to see a watch lying on the table.

ALEX
Bobby.

The PDA is at its highest vibration while Alex is holding Bobby's watch in his other hand. He then turns to his left to see a leg sticking out from the side of a desk. It's a man in a doctor's uniform. His lifeless body lies there with writing in blood seen on the wall: "Alex, City Park Zoo."

Alex activates his PDA's search and find. A location for City Park Zoo in the city shows up. Also written on the wall are numbers. He reads the numbers and starts to type them in. A bottle tips over and falls to the floor. Alex turns to see a four-legged creature, not more than eight inches long, standing on top of a table. It's brown with scales all over and gills on the side of its head. It stares at him and sniffs the air as Alex slowly pulls back his coat and unfastens his holster. The creature creeps a little bit closer.

Alex knows what's about to happen just as it gives off a short pitch scream before Alex shoots it down. The gun had a silencer to prevent from making as much noise as possible. After shooting down the creature, he hears movement throughout the air ducts with sounds of claws scratching the interior. A vent cover pops out and five more appears. Alex shoots down the 1st, but the 2nd knocks his gun out of his hand.

He throws a knife to take down the 3rd. He then pulls out another gun to finish off the 4th and 5th creature. This gun has no silencer on it. The scene changes to the outside of the office as three more gunshots echo throughout the hallway. The moaning begins making its way closer to Alex's location. He quickly gets back to the wall with the numbers and finishes typing them in. The PDA reacts by showing a red dot pulsing in the same area as the city zoo. Heading out of the office, he notices that the slimy veins are growing, covering where he originally came from.

Alex finds himself fighting off the dead in a meeting room set up for a banquet that never took place. That's when he's overwhelmed by more zombies crashing through the doors. He fires to both sides of him, but they keep getting closer, forcing him to climb on top of a table, continuing to reload.

One zombie leaps out of the crowd right at him and they both go crashing through the window.

Alex lands on a platform being held by cables. The zombie that fell with Alex gets tangled with a cord on the edge of the platform and is now hand by its neck struggling. Alex shoots the cord, sending the zombie falling through the fog. Alex sees no way to get to a window that isn't occupied by the undead. The thick veins begin to break through the sides of the building, making the structure of the hospital even more unstable. Alex looks at the cords holding the platform and back to the veins approaching his position. He aims his gun and fires. The platform drops a little.

A zombie falls on top of Alex. The dead are falling from above as the hospital continues to break apart. He fires at the zombie, sending it over the platform. As the thick vein goes for Alex's feet, he fires at the 3rd cord holding the platform and begins falling strait down. The thick fog clouds Alex's visibility as he's trying to hang on. He looks up to see more giant veins coming from above. Alex pulls out 2 sub-machine guns and begins firing. Slicing apart the veins, he looks down as the platform clears the fog.

Hordes of zombies appears below, snarling and moaning with their hands waving in the air as giant pieces of slabs of the building falls from above, crushing the zombies to the ground. Alex leaps into the air before hitting the ground and falls on top of a bolder after hitting the side of an abandon ambulance. He gets up with a little bit of blood dripping from his mouth as couple of zombies are at his feet, trying to get to their next meal. He just shoots them down and the building continues to fall as it's consumed by the giant veins. Holding his right side, Alex slowly walks away, leaving a giant tree-like structure behind where the hospital once stood.

Out in a foggy field, a figure is seen walking through the tall grass. We're seeing through the eyes of something as everything is in night vision mode. It's Alex, wearing a pair of black glasses that allows him to see through the darkness. Spotting a small structure in the distance, he decides to stop by to do a quick check. With no luck on opening the front door, Alex walks around to the side to see that the windows are boarded up. He peeks through and sees nothing. The sound of a twig being snapped is heard from behind. Alex quickly turns around to have a blinding light beam through his glasses.

Snatching off his glasses and rubbing his eyes, he hears a voice with a hint of an Irish accent.

                         COLONEL
                       Don't move.

     As his vision started to come back, a man completely bald
with a dark blue coat and black pants is standing in front of
him.

                         COLONEL
                What are you doing here, Alex?

                          ALEX
                Good to see you too, colonel.

                         COLONEL
                  You shouldn't be here.
          You should of returned with your team to HQ.

                          ALEX
                   You know about that?

                         COLONEL
                  We need to get inside.

     The colonel bangs on the front door in code.

                         COLONEL
                   It's OK! Open up!

     The door opens to a man in green pants and a wind- breaker.
Both the colonel and Alex enter. The Colonel closes the door
and puts the metal bar back in place to lock it back up. The
Colonel peeks through the cracks of the boarded up window
and sees nothing but fog covering the land. He then turns to
Alex.

                         COLONEL
     So what are you doing here? You were to report back with the
              rest of your team after the mission.

ALEX
Before the city was sterilized, I gathered information that the first outbreak was the work of an IPA scientist that went missing a year ago.

OWENS
Xavier Grounds.

ALEX
That's right. The information I found links him to a secret organization that was planning on using the nan-nites for a terror attack.

COLONEL
He was being forced to work with this group on the count that his family was being held captive. After learning this, there were two missions set forth:
1st send in a spy to infiltrate this mysterious organization.
2nd bring back Ground's family. IPA sent in a team for the rescue attempt, but his family was already dead. We were however successfully able to send in our mole, who have been leaking us information. An attack will take place in Georgia tomorrow. All available agents are assembling as we speak.

ALEX
What about us?

COLONEL
Soon as our mission is complete, our rescue will escort us to Georgia to assemble with the others. That's if we're successful. Doc, could you please keep an eye on our guest?

The colonel leaves the room in a hurry. Owens finishes the download on the laptop computer he was working on and puts the cord back into his shirt. He straightens himself and turns towards Alex.

OWENS
You must excuse the colonel. Giving the circumstances, well I'm sure you understand. I'm Owens by the way. I was sent here to collect samples for the agency.

ALEX
You're a Unit Droid.

OWENS
That's right.

ALEX
Trying to find a cure for the plague? Incase of another
outbreak.

OWENS
Well, better safe than sorry. I was hoping that my first
programmed assignment would have been a lot simpler.

Alex walks over to the table Owens was sitting at. Alex
looks to see a cylinder on the edge of the table, pulsing a
dim blue light.

ALEX
What are you doing?

OWENS
I was trying to access the lab's database from here. The
laptop connected to my internal modem isn't producing a
strong enough signal for me to do that.

Alex pulls out a disk.

ALEX
Would this help?

OWENS
Maybe. What is it?

ALEX
I found it in one of the labs. I was hoping to get
information about the mayor from this. It turns out that
Atlanta wasn't the origin of the virus.

Owens places the disk into the computer.

                    OWENS
           That's why you're here?

                    ALEX
Not exactly. I've been in contact with my kid brother. But
then the transmissions ended. So I was to meet up with an
  agency contact who was watching over my family. When I
  arrived, the contact was dead and Bobby was missing.

Alex pulls out his PDA.

                    ALEX
        I believe this is his new location.

                    OWENS
        The zoo. Strange place to be hiding.

Owens turns to the sound of the laptop beeping.

                    OWENS
It's encrypted. I can't get pass the embedded security. Who
      ever set this up did not want anyone near it.

  Owens pulls out the disk and gives it back to Alex, who was
holding the pulsing cylinder. The colonel enters the room with
a duffle bag.

                    OWENS
          Could you not touch that?

                    ALEX
            What is it?

COL. JOHNSON
A device that will help us get rid of the virus plaguing the
city.

Owens takes the cylinder from Alex and puts it back on the
table.

COL. JOHNSON
Doc, you have it?

OWENS
Not yet.

The colonel walks over to one of the boarded up windows to
peek outside.

ALEX
I tried to get access myself. But I didn't know that a code
was needed.

COL. JOHNSON
I know. The mayor was able to get a few laws passed,
including certain changes to the agency's security
systems. Pack up everything. We've got company.

The colonel is looking through the cracks of a window and
sees dark figures walking through the fog. The colonel turns
to Alex.

                    COL. JOHNSON
            I hope you're packing.

Alex pulls out one of his guns.

                    COL. JOHNSON
         They won't do. Here, take this.

The colonel gives Alex a modified P90 and a 9mm.

                      ALEX
          What kind of guns are these?

                    COL. JOHNSON
   New models developed by our scientists. Check out the
      bullets. Specially made with an electromagnetic
        cells within each bullet to act as an EMP.
         It's designed to shut down the nan-nites.

                      ALEX
         Nice. I could of use this yesterday.

Owens walks over with his stuff.

                    OWENS
                Ok. Lets go.

                  COL. JOHNSON
                To the back.

    The three of them make their way to exit out the back of the
cabin. You can see the shadows of the dead creeping towards the
boarded up cabin with moaning sounds.

    Out in the woodland area, the colonel and Owens are both
walking down a path ahead as Alex is trailing behind, impatiently
looking at his PDA.

                    ALEX
        You still didn't tell me on how did you
            know about my team in sector 5K

                  COL. JOHNSON
    Your Unit Droid was able to download you entire mission to
headquarters, which then was sent to me. The agency was also
    able to monitor all other communications on the island.
    Including a short transmission sent out by you brother.

                    ALEX
            So you know where Bobby is?

                  COL. JOHNSON
Something shorted out the com-link. We weren't able to get a
fix on his location or the agent that was keeping an eye on
                  your family.

                    ALEX
The agency sent in a team. Then they must of known about the
            operation going on here.

                  COL. JOHNSON
About a day ago they went in, we lost transmission. The last
 one reported the appearance of the mayor in the city. They
were to bring him in for some questioning about the incident
in Atlanta. Soon as we lost communications, I was sent in to

do a quick investigation myself and get three transmitters up
and running for the sterilization process.

                          ALEX
                      Transmitters?
                The cylinder I was holding?

                       COL. JOHNSON
     Yes. It's for the satellite's targeting system. It'll help
           the beam to hit its target through the storm.

                          ALEX
                  Then I can't go with you.

                       COL. JOHNSON
                         Why not?

                          ALEX
                   I need to find Bobby.

                       COL. JOHNSON
     Not to sound cruel, but it's best to except the possibility
                  that you brother is dead.

                          ALEX
     I kept getting a signal from him on my way to the island. I
     also found a message from the agent assigned to my family to
                  meet Bobby at the city zoo.

     The colonel stops and turns to Alex.

                       COL. JOHNSON
     Seeing how you're not officially part of my mission, I'm not
            going to try and force you to come with us.

     The colonel takes Alex's PDA and starts to type into it. He
     then hands it back.

                       COL. JOHNSON
     You have to understand. If you're not at the lighthouse, in
     this location when the chopper arrives, you're going to be on
                   this island when the beam hits.

ALEX
I understand. I'll meet up with you later.

Alex cuts through a different path in the woods, leaving the colonel and Owens behind.

COL. JOHNSON
All right, lets get moving.

The scene changes to Alex pushing away twigs, making his way to an open area. Coming up to a side gate, he starts to climb the wall and jumps over the edge. A small structure is in his view. "City Park Zoo Security Office" is written on the side of the structure. The thunder claps gets stronger. No rain falls, but the air is dry. Alex walks around the office building to see the front door open with no signs of life. He turns and begins walking towards the front gate of the zoo to find that it is locked with a dead bolt.

ALEX
Bobby, I hope you're safe.

A zombie leaps at the chained gate with a loud roar. The gate rattles loudly as the walking corps is desperately trying to get to its fresh meal. It roars even louder as if it was trying to summon something to its location. Alex backs up to the security office, not sure what to do about the dozens of zombies appearing out of the shadow. Where there was a couple dozen, now over a hundred. They began piling over one another to reach the top of the gate.

The bolts holding the gates together starts to buckle and Alex turns East to see a wide open area to run to. Suddenly a corpse crashes through the window and tries to pull Alex inside. He breaks free and fires off a few rounds. A huge fireball rises to the sky out in the far distance, causing a mushroom cloud to form out in the East.

The zoo gates falls to the ground spewing the dead all over the place. Other corpses continue to leap from the shadows of the forest and heads for Alex. They are also coming through a small entrance on the right side. Alex pulls out a gun that the colonel gave him and begins firing. The bullets are giving off a blue light as they just about to hit their targets. Everything goes to slow motion as we can see a bullet leave the barrel of the gun. Parts on the bullet starts to move and spin. You hear these parts connect and a blue light is lit. Everything speeds up for a second until it hit a zombie's head, then is shown shutting down the nan-nites with the EMP it's emitting, bringing the zombie to the ground after the bullet emerges from the back of the head and hits a propane tank.

An explosion occurs, taking out 60 corpses near the small gateway. That's when Alex hears a very loud roar coming from the woods straight ahead. Trees are being knocked down as something huge is coming towards the zoo. Alex bends down and opens his duffle bag to grab a disk with a dome on both sides. He presses the domes to activate the device as the giant creature gets closer. The disk is tossed just in time, causing and explosion of light, taking out the zombies at the main gate and sending this shadowy creature hurling backwards. A close up of the zombies shows torsos eagerly trying to make their way to Alex's position. He gathers his things and heads East with zombies howling into the wind.

Scene changes with bodies flying backwards through the air and falling to the ground with bullet holes all over them. The bodies gets back up while the rest of the dead are being attacked by soldiers in red, appearing and disappearing as they fire everything they have. Alex comes around the corner to see soldiers and zombies slaughtering each other. A figure can be seen in a crouched position surrounded by a couple of soldiers firing in all directions.

Keeping his distance to view all the action, Alex doesn't notice something approaching from behind. He turns around and barely escapes the swing of a giant claw. With no effect of his gunfire, the creature roars more and continues towards its prey.

Not being able to take down this bear-like monster, he's forced to run directly into the battle itself. One of the soldiers notices the creature and a man running in their direction and alerts the rest of the team on his wristband. That's when mutations, once star attractions of the city zoo, begins showing up and knocking down the zombies to get to the soldiers.

                    LEADER (human-robotic voice)
            The cloaking device isn't fooling the
              animals. We got to get out of here.

The fight gets more intense as deformed zoo creatures are tearing everyone apart. The soldier's numbers are quickly dwindled to a handful. A monster of an elephant leaps over other animals and lands on top a couple of the soldiers. It has skin like an armadillo, paws like a cat, and fangs like a saber-tooth tiger. It tosses zombies and soldiers into the air as 3 soldiers fires off grenade rounds to finally take the beast down.

The ground starts to tremble with rocks from crumbling walls falling to the ground. A huge piece of the ground starts to rise in front of everyone, trapping them in a circle of debris. It's a tail end of something appearing as more of the ground begins to rise, circling the soldiers as the ground breaks away more. It's a giant snake with the head of a king cobra and mandibles all over its face and a stinger on its tail. One of the soldiers has a small canon on his arm and fires at the snake. It explodes in half and lies there lifeless.

                         SOLDIER-6
                 That was easy enough.

   The two parts of the giant snake begins wobbling and the end piece with the missing tail re-grows a tail along with the piece with the missing head re-growing its head. There are now 2 of these giant snakes. The remaining soldiers starts to fire. You can tell something is different about these soldiers, not only by their voice, but one of the bigger ones has bullet shells popping out of it side as he fires. As one of the snakes slithers in Alex's direction, a giant harry spike slams the snake into the ground. Molten lava begins dripping from above. The snake is lifted up and slammed into the ground a second time. Everyone looks up to see an eight-legged beast of massive size and strength, with lava spewing from its jaws, taking out everything around it. The 2nd snake goes after the Magma Spider for an attack. The 1st snake that was slammed into the ground breaks into two and now there are 3 snakes fighting with the spider.

   One of the snakes gets near the spider's mouth and is crushed by its massive jaws, causing more snakes to appear. Where there were 2 snakes, there are now 10. The Magma Spider roars out load as its body expands in size and spews out fire and magma out of its mouth like a flamethrower. It spins around in circles out of control killing zombies, zoo mutations and some of the soldiers that are on the ground. The flame makes its way around towards Alex, who is trying to catch up with the others. Alex sees the flames breaking down the structure of the zoo and the mysterious figure was in the way.

                          ALEX
                         Bobby!

                    BOBBY
                    Alex?

                    ALEX
              Bobby, are you ok?

                    LEADER
           Lets go! Lets go! Lets go!

They all make it through an opening that leads to a cavern
as the leader of the soldiers and Alex turns around to hold off
the remaining corpses that were trying to catch up with them.
Leader takes his machine gun in one hand and fires along the
legs of the zombies to take them to the ground. Knowing that
they can't hold the horde off too long, Alex and Leader heads
into the cave. The zombies enter the entrance, stepping on a
flashing device that was left behind. The device goes off.
BOOM! The screen is filled with dirt and smoke as the scene
changes.

The smoke and dirt turns to fog and clears with Owens looking
upon a shopping mall that is boarded up from the inside. The
colonel is at the windows to see that they were boarded up as
well. Shopping carts are scattered all over the parking lot
near abandon cars

                    OWENS
            Looks like they failed at
               keeping things out.

                    COLONEL
              Any life-signs?

                    OWENS
         I can't pick up anything. That doesn't
         mean that we're not going in, does it?

                    COLONEL
           The second transmitter can be
               placed on the roof.

They both begin climbing to the roof. The scene changes to the edge of the roof and hands appears as both the colonel and Owens make their way over. The colonel gets to the center, leaving Owens back at the edge. He takes a look at his wristband as it guides him to the precise location to place the transmitter.

                         OWENS
                    Everything ok?

The colonel responds with static on the radio caused by the electric field in the sky.

                         COLONEL
                  Yeah, Don't worry.
                The line-a-sight will work.

After unpacking the equipment, the colonel begins attaching parts for the second transmitter together. That's when he stops to the sound of crackling beneath his feet. Owens notices Johnson walking strangely. Owens looks down to the roof to see the structural integrity weakening.

                         OWENS
                       Colonel?

                         COLONEL
                I know. Get back to the ground!

The roof begins to collapse in the middle, taking the colonel and the transmitter inside the mall. Seeing that the middle part of the roof was unstable, Owens carefully walks over to the edge of the cave-in.

                         OWENS
                 Colonel! Can you hear me?

Johnson sits up with his hand over a cut on the side of his head. He then gets to his feet as he clears some of the rubble away. He looks to his left and sees the transmitter under stairs and walks over to it.

                        COLONEL
          Well, at least it's still transmitting.

He picks up the transmitter and placed it were he fell. He then gets out his flashlight and starts searching for a way out of the mall.

                        OWENS
                      Colonel?

                        COLONEL
          Look, the transmitter is still transmitting.
          See if you can help me find a way out of here.

                        OWENS
                    I'm on it.

Owens knows that there was no way to get the colonel out through the roof, so he makes his way down to the ground to see if there was an opening. Meanwhile, the colonel has entered another room with no luck of a way out. He then grabs a small device out of his pocket. The Colonel runs into a man and a woman with food in their hands.

                        MATT
                Whoa! Don't shoot!

                        COLONEL
          I'm not going to shoot. Just calm down.
              Are there anymore of you?

                        MATT
              Me, my wife, April, and
                a handful of others.

A loud rumble is felt along the walls of the mall.

                    MATT
          Is that thunder?

                    APRIL
          No, not thunder.

                    MATT
          Than what was it?

The colonel makes sure his weapon is fully loaded.

                    COLONEL
          You need to take me to the others.

                    MATT
          Right this way.

The colonel, Matt, and April arrive at a bank vault with busted hinges on the door. Matt pounds on the door. The door opens to show us three more survivors. Harold, a 60 year old man bandaged up with a missing arm, Reda, an older woman with a nursing background, and a ten year old boy.

                    COLONEL
          We got survivors, Doc.

The colonel gets nothing but static in his ear-piece.

                    COLONEL
          How many survivors do
          we have here?

                    APRIL
      Well, there's us five and MJ's parents,
        who should be on their way back.

Suddenly a loud bang hit the wall to right. Another bang. Then silence. The sound of something crawling emerges all around him. The wall begins to rattle and objects falls to the floor with glass shattering everywhere. Silence.

                         COLONEL
                You all stay inside and
                   close the door.

The colonel continues to make his way to the other end of the mall. Sensing that something was watching him, he continues down the dark hallway with his flashlight and customized Winchester at hand. A wall to his side gives away, revealing two giant harry worms with scorpion-like legs and huge mouths, getting in his way to the doors at the back of the mall

The creatures begins to charge the colonel and he starts firing his weapon, spitting out the same EMP bullets Alex was given, as he heads into another room. The creatures can be heard from behind roaring as loud as they can. The colonel is back into an open area leaving the two creatures behind. Something falls to the floor grabbing his attention. It was a corpse getting up from a corner, and it looked hungry. Then another one rises from behind the guest service counter. Now nine more appears.

A zombie leaps from behind, but is shot down from gunfire. The colonel looks to his left to see a tall man in long black braids and a goatee, wearing camo gear, holding a shotgun in his hand, firing off rounds with a woman who is equally tall with jet black hair, wearing jeans and a tank top. All three continue to fire until the last corpse is down. The tall man turns to the colonel as he catches his breath.

                         MARCUS
                Where's the rest of you?

                         COLONEL
                The rest of me?

                        MARCUS
            What, you're not the rescue team
                 that never showed up?

    The colonel ejects the empty clip from his Winchester and
reloads, knowing that there's still danger coming.

                        COLONEL
              There's no rescue team
                 coming for you.

                        MARCUS
                 No rescue team?
            Then who the hell are you?

    A loud bang hits the wall from the other side with a deep
low growl. All three ready their weapons. A second bang creates
large cracks followed by a third bang. After a few seconds of
silence, the wall gives away as one of the worm creatures rushes
through. The ceiling gives away and the other worm creature
falls through and onto one of the escalators, roaring loudly.
The tall woman looks to a little boy carrying a book bag.

                        ANGELINA
                M.J., get back!

    The little boy runs back into the vault from which he came and
everyone continues firing their weapons in hopes to take down
the two beasts, but it's not looking good for our survivors.

                        MARCUS
                  Screw this!

    Marcus pulls out a grenade, pops the pin, and throws it into
the far right background at the worm that was circling around
for a kill. The explosion brings down the escalators and falls
onto the wounded beast.

Owens himself, unsuccessfully able to find another way in, comes around the corner to see an explosion coming from the back of the mall, knocking him to the ground. The colonel slowly gets to his feet. As does Marcus, Angelina, and everyone else. Angelina looks to her left and to her right.

                    ANGENLINA
                    M.J?
                    M.J!

                    M.J.
               I'm here. Over here.

M.J. slowly makes his way over the rubble coughing up the smoke from his mouth.

                    ANGELINA
                    M.J.

She runs to him and holds him tight in her arms, relieved that he's still alive. M.J. struggles a little.

                    M.J.
               I can't breath.

                    MARCUS
               Angie, you're going to
                 suffocate the boy.

Angie loosens her grip on her son.

                    OWENS
           I see we have survivors.

                    COLONEL
             A total of seven.
             Is everyone ok?

MATT
Just peachy.

REDA
H, you all right?
How's your arm?

HAROLD
I'm still missing it.

MARCUS
HA! Good one, H.

The Colonel checks his watch to see that the transmitter is still in place and active.

COLONEL
Come on. We have one
last place to go.

The colonel turns to the others.

COLONEL
We have to hurry to our last destination
before a rescue chopper arrives.

MARCUS
You said that there wasn't
a rescue team coming.

COLONEL
I said there wasn't a rescue coming
for you. But one is on its way for the
Doc and I. You all are welcome to join us.

APRIL
We're not going to say no to that.

Everyone gets together and follows the colonel and Owens to the lighthouse.

Alex, Bobby, and the remaining soldiers emurged out of the woods to the front of the lighthouse. As they are about to make their way through the tall wall of twigs, one of the soldiers holds out his arms to stop Alex. As Alex is stopped, the arm of Leader starts to become invisible. The other 4 soldiers began to cloak as well. Alex and Bobby just stand there as you can see the invisible soldiers walk through the twigs and tall bushes.

Suddenly you hear gunfire and zombies roaring. Light is flickering from the gunfire and bullets shreds through the bushes, causing Alex and Bobby to get to the ground. Now there is silence. As Alex slowly gets back up, the head of a zombie comes rushing through the twigs to attack, but and invisible hand grabs the corps at the mouth from behind and drags it out of the scene. A couple of lights flicker as the soldier fires into it.

                    LEADER
              It's ok. You two can
               come out now.

The scene changes to outside of the bushes where you can see a large open field where the soldiers are de-cloaking as they stand by the sides of the dead. Alex and Bobby make their way through to look up to see a light-house. The sky is still thick with grey clouds and bits of thunder rumbling.

                    ALEX
            So, you guys are here for the
         transport that's picking up the colonel?

The soldiers look up at each other.

                    LEADER
         Yeah, it should be here soon.
       We just have to get to the lab first.

One of the soldiers comes up to their leader.

                   SOLDIER-2
           We can't find the entrance.

                    LEADER
          Then we are going the other way.

    The soldiers, Alex, and Bobby make their way to the entrance
of the lighthouse. The inside was made of stones with a spiral
formation, including the stairs. One of the soldiers spotted
drips of blood on the floor leading around the corner. He
follows the trail and discovers a man in a blue outfit very
much like his. The muscle mass is protruding from the armor
in a horrific way. Looks as if the man was suffering before
death.

                    LEADER
                 What is it?

                   SOLDIER-3
         I don't know. This can't be good
     if he's here. There could be more of them.

                    LEADER
         We can't worry about that now.
         We've got a mission to complete.

                   SOLDIER-2
          Hey. You two coming or not?

    The two soldiers get to their feet and follow the rest up the
spiral stairs to the top of the lighthouse. The scene changes
to the interior of the top of the lighthouse. A hatch on the
floor opens and one of the soldiers slowly makes his way in to
make sure the area was secured.

SOLDIER-4
All clear.

The rest makes their way through and begins looking around
as one of the soldiers notices a pulsing blue light on a corner
shelf.

SOLDIER-3
Hey, over here.

ALEX
It's a 3 dimensional transmitter.

Soldier-3 leans over to leader.

SOLDIER-3
Others were definitely here.

Another soldier is clicking on a keyboard trying to access
the computer. Alex turns to the sound coming from the giant
column in the middle of the room. A door opens up on the front
of the column, revealing and elevator.

LEADER
Move in.

The elevator door closes and the scene changes to the inside
of a giant sewer with caverns going in different directions.
A manhole cover is being pride open from above with a light
shining through followed by voices.

COLONEL
All right. We're going down.

One by one the 9 of them climbs down into the smelly area.
Angelina sees a dead sewer worker decomposed as it is wedged

through the wide cracks of the wall and has to keep her mouth
tightly closed. M. J. notices the body as well.

                    M.J.
                    Cool

                    MARCUS
            That's my boy. Keeping his
            head up in a world where
            everything wants to eat him.

    They are at the bottom, looking at the sewer water standing
still and roaches crawling across the walls.

                    COLONEL
            There are two ways to go, Doc.

    We get a close up look at Owens' eyes as the pupils adjust
themselves giving Owens a grid of the sewers for them to plan
their route.

                    OWENS
            Our way to the lab is that way.

                    ANGELINA
            Why are we going to a lab?

                    COLONEL
            The Doc. and I are looking for
            a man who is directly related to
            the nightmare you're living in.
            We get to him, we could end all of this.

                    MARCUS
            It has something to do with those
            machines people were putting into their
            bodies to loose weight, isn't it.

                    HAROLD
        What ever happened to good old
               fashion exercise?

Harold coughs up blood with a chuckle.

                     M.J.
              What was that?

Marcus raises his shotgun and flashlight. Owens touches the
side of his ear and we can hear a click.

                    OWENS
        We won't be able to go any further.

                    COLONEL
               Detour?

     Owens looks around a little.

                    OWENS
               The door ahead.

     All 9 are quickly making their way behind Owens. Splashing
sounds is rapidly being made ahead of them. They all stop as
the colonel is at the door, not able to open it. There is a
panel with a numerical keypad.

     The splashing gets closer as if there were many things in the
water with them running in their direction. Owens was the first
to fire off a few rounds. The others gather together as the kid
gets behind them. A zombie comes running out from the darkness.
The colonel is still at the door, still trying to bust it open.
As they continue to fire, a few more zombies raises out of the
water behind them.

                    M.J.
               Behind us!

     Angelina and April fires in one direction while Marcus and
Matt fires in the other. Owens fires in both directions with
a gun in each hand as the sewer tunnels are being lit up in
blue and orange lights. Marcus looks down one of the tunnels
and sees dozens of flickering lights closing in on their
position.

                    MARCUS
               What the hell is that?

     Giant fire flies appears out of the darkness quickly passing
by the few zombies in the water and begins swarming around
everyone.

ANGELINA
I'm running out of ammo here!

Owens pulls out a gun and tosses it.

OWENS
Make it count.

She turns around and fires, with a blue light from the bullets, sends 2 zombies backwards. A squiggly monster riser in front of Marcus and knocks him towards the Colonel, who is unsuccessfully to getting open the door even with gunfire. The squiggly monster sees M.J., but Owens steps in between them and punches the monster in its chest, knocking it far away into the other zombies. Marcus gets to his feet and looks at the door.

MARCUS
Get the hell out of the way!

Marcus makes a run for it. He slams into the door and bounces back into the sewer water and rises up, gasping for air as gunfire is commencing all around him. The Colonel looks at the door to see that Marcus was able to bust it open a little. He then gives it a good kick.

COLONEL
Lets move it!

They all go through the door and tries to slam it shut, but a corpse's arm is keeping it from closing completely. Owens is holding the door as the Colonel and Marcus bring over a log to block the zombies out. They are in total darkness and we hear a clicking sound coming from Owens.

OWENS
Everyone reload, now.

Everyone starts to reload while Owens views their surroundings with night vision to show us dead construction workers and lab technicians standing before them. The colonel ignites a flare and tosses it far in front of the group to show the survivors what waits for them. The dead begins slowly making their way towards everyone and steps on the flare the colonel threw, making it pitch black again.

                    MARCUS
              SONE OF A BITCH!

The firefight lights up the area with images of the dead being torn apart. Angelina looks around for her son.

                    ANGELINA
              Buddy, stay close!

                    COLONEL
              Owens, get us out of here.

Owens shoots off a flare of his own that leaves a green glowing liquid, making a trail for everyone to follow down a lower stair case.

                    OWENS
              That way.

Everyone sees the green light and follows Owens from behind, fighting off the hordes of the living dead at the same time. A short scream is heard as survivors are being picked off. Owens turns to see something with wings swooping by, taking out someone else.

                    OWENS
              Hurry up!

Everyone moves faster while Owens stays behind watching winged creatures circling around for another kill. He sees Reda about to be snatched up, so he fires a single shot to the head of the creature. It falls right behind her as she freezes in fear.

                    OWENS
              Come on. It's ok.

Reda moves closer towards Owens, but is stopped by two spears protruding through her chest and stomach. Owens looks upon to see the woman being lifted up in the air by the now headless winged creature as it mutates into something else.

                    REDA
              Go! Get out of here!

Owens turns back towards the others to catch up with them. We are now being lead to a maintenance area. We see a marble brick area with the looks of a storage room for large cargo with maintenance tools on top of boxes next to an elevator. There's a frail skinny zombie wearing a maintenance uniform, slowly walking around, moaning for something to eat. A clanking sound is being made from the other side of a circular gate that leads to a dark tunnel.

The zombie walks to the vertical bars. Once it got right to the gate, Owens' arms comes through and grabs it, pulling it's head through the bars. You hear a snapping sound and the zombie slides to the ground. Owens' then grabs the bars and bends them open. They all walk through the gate and into the cargo area. Getting around the corpse, they make it to the elevator. The colonel clicks the up button, with no response.

                    COLONEL
              Is this all there is?

                    OWENS
              Looks like it. Maybe they
              should of stayed up top and
              waited for the chopper.

                    COLONEL
          They would have been exposed in
          the open with no beacon. Sadly,
          they were better off with us.

     The colonel tries out the elevator with no luck. He then
turns to Owens expecting a solution to their new problem.

                    COLONEL
          The elevator's not responding.

                    OWENS
          No power?

     Owens sees a circuit board near the control panel for the
elevator.

                    OWENS
          I should be able to communicate
          with the computer and get
          the elevators working.

     Owens sits down against the wall right under the panel.
He then presses the back of his neck, which opens a small
panel, revealing advance circuitry not yet seen by the public.
The colonel kneels down beside Owens and pulls out a cable
and begins attaching it directly into the elevator's control
panel.

                    OWENS
          Accessing . . . who ever put this
          system together really knew what
          they were doing.

                    COLONEL
          You can get through. Right?

                    OWENS
          Shouldn't be a problem.

Marcus notices the zombie at the gate starting to move. So he takes the gun Angelina got from Owens, walks over and fires at it. The power light on the elevator buttons comes on.

> COLONEL
> Good. It's on.
> Lets get you up.

> OWENS
> No, I can't. There's no power source
> spreading to the elevators.
> You're going to have to leave me.

Knowing that he can't disagree, the colonel checks his watch.

> COLONEL
> We're in the right location.
> But I'm not sure if I'm going
> to get it to the top.

> OWENS
> Than we're going to have to hope
> the satellite picks it up from down here.

The colonel hands Owens the transmitter. The elevator doors opens and Marcus and his family enters, followed by the colonel.

> COLONEL
> Will you be able to upload your data?

> OWENS
> Only time will tell.

The colonel enters and the elevator doors closes.

The scene changes to a set of doors of a giant column opens. Alex and Bobby comes out behind the 5 remaining soldiers into an area with train tracks leading north of their position. On the east and west of the elevator are two giant oval openings with no tracks leading to other parts of the underground area.

> LEADER
> You two, head down there.
> You two, east entrance.
> You all have 15 minutes
> to report back.

Four of the soldiers split into two teams and heads down the two entrances. Leader walks over to the north entrance that has a locked door. Giant and oval as well, but password protected.

> LEADER
> Stay here.

Leader sees a hole for a special type of circular key by the panel to the keypad. He sticks his finger into it and numbers starts to systematically flicker until the door opens. The area on the other side was dark with flickering lights.

    Soldier 2 and 3 enter into an area still under construction. There are stair rails all over the place, leading to a lower platform and to a higher platform. Giant containers with the symbol for flammable chemical are a lined along the wall.

SOLDIER-2
Those canisters must be applying fuel
to something. You take the lower half.
See if any of those doors leads to anywhere.
I'll check out the office on top.

As soldier-2 makes his way up to the office on the top floor, soldier-3 looks down at the broken stairway. He pulls out a gun with a rope attached to it and drops down. He lets go of the gun still attached to the upper stairway and immediately makes his way to one of the two doors.

                         SOLDIER-3
                         Locked, eh?

Soldier-3 rams his fist through the wooden door and swings the door all the way open with his gun raised. It was an empty broom closet with cleaning supplies. Soldier-3 turns to the other door. Also locked and made of steel. He was also able to ram his fist through. This time the door doesn't budge. He looks to the lining of the door and notices burn marks. The door has been torched shut. He bends down and looks through the hole where the doorknob use to be.

                         SOLDIER-2
                         Anything?

                         SOLDIER-3
                          Nothing.

                         SOLDIER-2
                      I found something.

Soldier-2 walks over to a dead body sitting in a chair at a computer terminal with blood all over the desk and a bullet hole in the back of the skull.

                         SOLDIER-2
                   There's a dead scientist
                     here at a computer.

Soldier-2 pushes the body aside and begins typing onto the keypad.

> SOLDIER-2
> Looks like he was trying to send
> and e-mail to someone. Looks like
> someone didn't want any information to get out.

The scene changes to the west entrance. A room filled with tubes containing specimens and cryo-chambers.

> SOLDIER-4
> Don't touch anything.

Soldier-5 is walking around large tubes standing vertically, filled with watery substance and creatures still alive, swimming around. Soldier-4 is taking blood samples from the zombies who were still frozen on the floor.

> SOLDIER-5
> Come on. They're inactive.

> SOLDIER-4
> These are, yes.
> But those still swimming
> around are the ones I'm
> concerned about.

Soldier-5 is rubbing the glass part of a cryo-tube filled with a clear liquid to see a creature asleep in a fetal position. Its arms and legs jerks a little.

> SOLDIER-5
> Big baby.

Soldier-4 finishes taking what little bit of the blood samples he could get and packs it away in his pouch.

> SOLDIER-4
> Ok. I got what we need.

Blood splatters onto soldier-4 and onto the wall. He turns around to see a creature, making its way through a hole in the ceiling, with a bottom half of what might be a snake and an upper half of a deformed man. It has soldier-5 in its mouth and chomps down breaking him in half. Soldier-4 begins firing. The gun firing alerts everyone. In the east side, soldier-2 and 3 leaps down from the office. Alex and Leader in the main section aimed their weapons to the west entrance where the gunfire is coming from.

SOLDIER-4
Get back! Get back!
I can't stop it!

Everyone begin backing up away from the west entrance as soldier-4 is coming out. Just as he makes it out of the tunnel, the monster's tongue hits him from behind and pulls him backing, followed by a loud roar.

The monster makes its way through eyeing its preys and drool dripping from its mouth. It slithers closer and closer to the group. Soldier-2 and soldier-3 comes from the east entrance. Soldier-2 fires a grenade round at the monster, but it leaps into the air, allowing the grenade to make its way into the cryo-chamber.

The monster is in mid air ready to land on soldier-2 and 3, but soldier-3 has already launched a grenade round himself, taking the upper body of the monster off. It slams to the floor with blood oozing all over. BOOM! An explosion comes from the cryo-room. Red lights and sounds start to go off. Back in the east room, canisters are pushed away from the wall by robotic arms. A woman's voice is heard over the intercom.

COMPUTER
Warning. Bio containment has been breached.
Commencing section b-1 lockdown immediately.

Doors to the east and west side begins to close, followed by the door Leader opened for the north entrance.

                              LEADER
                           Follow me!

    They all make it through the north entrance before the door
closes. The steel door closes with a loud explosion coming
from behind. They can hear a pounding on the other side, then
silence. One of the soldiers activates a trolley they found
themselves on and proceed forward.

    A circular door opens and a trolley enters with its passengers
into what appears to be security area. With a giant computer
terminal and monitors along the wall. Nearby are two elevators
and a door with the words Administrative Director, Paul Newton
engraved. Alex walks over to the door of Paul Newton and begins
punching in random codes to open the door. The Leader shakes
his head and speaks sarcastically.

                              LEADER
                   What, you don't know the code?

    Leader opens the door the same way he opened the north
entrance door.

                              LEADER
                   You two stay here and see what
                   you can do about the main power.

    Leader, Alex, and Bobby enters the room and door closes from
behind. The other two soldiers make their way to the giant
computer monitors.

                             SOLDIER-2
                        This won't be easy.

    The scene changes to Newton's office. The floor is carpeted
in this barely furnished room. Ahead of them is a computer desk
with a fake window above. To the left is a restroom that Leader
checks out while Alex is at the computer trying to access data
files. Alex pulls out his disk he got from a lab in Atlanta.

                    LEADER
             Can you hack in?

Alex responds sarcastically.

                    ALEX
         What, you don't know the code.

                    LEADER
           Not without a keyhole.

                    ALEX
         Depends on the security system.

Alex puts the disk in. Everything seems to be going well.
Suddenly, the light goes out.

                    ALEX
             What happened?

Scene changes back to the security area with the other two
soldiers who are trying to solve the problem.

                  COMPUTER
        Intruder alert. Intruder alert.
         Commencing security lockdown.

                  SOLDIER-3
             That's not good.

Back in Newton's office, the Leader is trying to get the
door to open.

                    LEADER
        The door won't budge and I can't get
             into contact with the others.

Alex is still at the computer with Bobby.

                    ALEX
        I can't pass the security.

Alex feels something brush by him.

                    ALEX
          Bobby, stop moving.
            Hey soldier.

                    LEADER
    Don't move. I thought I heard something.

    Leader holds his gun tightly in his hands and starts to walk
to the bathroom.

                    ALEX
                  Anything?

    BOOM! The sound of something busting through the wall of the
bathroom is heard. Bobby clicks on a mini flashlight he had on
him. Alex takes it and heads towards the bathroom.

                    BOBBY
              Where is he?

                    ALEX
                  Gone.

                    BOBBY.
              So what now?

    Alex slowly walks into the bathroom. He gets closer to the
hole in the wall with Bobby's flashlight. He then slowly peeks
through and sees a sewer system. Looking up, Alex notices

webbing near the hole and throughout the passageway. He turns back for Bobby to try and find a way to the other end of the sewer system. That is when a clicking sound is heard from the other side of the office door.

                    ALEX
              Bobby, get around the
              corner and stay there.

   Bobby does as he's told as Alex aims his gun to whatever what ever may come through. It's the Colonel with Marcus and his family standing behind.

ALEX
You're not dead.

COLONEL
Not yet.
You made it here all by yourself?

ALEX
The other soldiers aren't there?

COLONEL
The only thing out here was this.

The colonel tosses a red hand that belonged to one of the other two soldiers. The computer continues to sound off intruder alert.

COMPUTER
Commencing self-destruct
in three minutes.

COLONEL
We're running out of time here.
Did you get the information you needed?

ALEX
No. I was unsuccessful.

Alex turns to the computer and quickly goes to it. He pushes the eject button to eject the disk he had put in. Nothing came out. Alex picks up the external CD-Rom drive and breaks it open. The disk was gone.

ALEX
The disk is gone.
The one I brought with me
to the island.

Everyone turns to the sound of the computer voice.

COMPUTER
Warning . . . second stage of bio-containment
has now been initiated. Self-destruct
will commence in two minutes.

MARCUS
This mission of yours is
about to get worst.

COLONEL
We can't go back the way we came.

ALEX
We're going to have to try and make
it through the tunnel. Maybe we'll
find out way out this way.

COMPUTER
Self-destruct will commence
in ninety seconds.

COLONEL.
After you.

ALEX
Bobby, follow behind me.

They all quickly head into the bathroom and through the hole
in the wall and start jogging down the tunnel.

COMPUTER
Warning . . . self-destruct will
commence in thirty seconds.

MARCUS
We can count, you dumb bitch!

ANGELINA
I'm not seeing any exits.

                    COMPUTER
        Warning . . . self-destruct will
        commence in fifteen seconds.

                     MARCUS
          We should of had stayed
              at the damn mall.

All six of them run into a dead end.

                    COMPUTER
                   10... 9...

Marcus holds his family in his arms as Bobby grabs ahold of
his big brother.

                    COMPUTER
             5... 4... 3... 2... 1...

Nothing happens. Everyone lets go of each other.

                      ALEX
                 What happened?

                    COLONEL
                  We didn't die.

Marcus sighs in relief and leans against the wall. He
activates a hidden panel and a door opens, revealing a tunnel
that is lit in a bright blue light.

                    COLONEL
          This must be our way out.

                    ANGELINA
            Is anyone else getting
              tired of tunnels?

ALEX
Lets get out of here.

One by one, they enter the tunnel of light as the door
starts to close behind them. The scene changes to an outside
field with the rain and thunder subsiding, leaving only strong
wind. The camera is focused on a manhole cover located in a
fenced-in area. It pops open and a hand moves it to the side.
Out comes the colonel, followed by Bobby, Alex, and the rest.
They look to see a tall fence with a locked gate and a view of
a long field leading to the sea. Behind them are the streets of
Charish Port with a cemetery near by. The colonel is looking
into the distance and sees where the edge of the ground end and
the ocean begins.

COLONEL
I can see the shore from here.

ALEX
My boat is tied up at the dock.

COLONEL
Then that's our way off this island.
We can send out a homing beacon to the
chopper from the waters.

The colonel takes the head of his gun and breaks the rusted
lock that kept the gates closed. All of them are now making
there way across the wooden bridge to get aboard Alex's armored
vessel.

ALEX
I'll get it started.

As Alex climbs up to the controls, the colonel looks around
at the boat Alex arrived on, checking out the cargo and the
guns on the side.

COLONEL
This isn't one of ours.
Where did you get it?

ALEX
At an oil refinery. After getting
Separated from my team, I found
this in an underground bunker.

Alex starts the engine and everyone sits securely as they move away from the island and out to ocean. The wind is slightly blowing while everyone has a sense of security as they leave the island and back to America.

The colonel is in the front of the boat checking his wristband. A couple of beeps goes off as he's moving patterns alone the touch screen with his finger. He then looks up towards Alex, who is busy steering.

COLONEL
Owens has been successfully
uploaded back to H.Q.

Another sound is coming from the device and we leave the boat upward through the clouds and to space where a satellite has just slowed down its speed to match the rotation of the earth. Parts start to come out and extend back, revealing 3 steel rods. They begin to heat up, emitting a green static charge. The colonel turns and walks over to see everyone sitting down.

COLONEL
You all might want to turn
around and take a look.

Everyone turns in the directions of the island to see a beam of green light piercing through the clouds, hitting the city, causing it to illuminate in a green glow. The colonel turns back around to the front and notices a light in the sky blinking within the clouds.

ALEX
Looks like our rescue arrived.

COLONEL

Do you have a radio on this boat?

ALEX

Yeah, it's up here.

The colonel makes his way to the boat's radio and tries to contact the chopper.

COLONEL
This is J Beta 426A62.
Do you copy? I repeat,
this J Beta 4262A62, come
in, over.

ALEX
Nothing?

COLONEL
No. the signal is going out,
but, I'm getting no response.

ALEX
Any idea what it is?

COLONEL
If it was our transport,
they'd would of responded.

Back on the boat, Bobby is at back at the edge of the boat and looks over into the far distance of the ocean. He notices a dark object approaching from behind. It starts to move faster followed by 5 small waves.

BOBBY
Alex!

Everyone turns to see something heading towards them. As the waves get closer, everyone stands in fear. Out of the water are dolphins, splashing about as they follow behind. A sigh of relief is heard. Bobby and M.J. are at the edge just looking at these beautiful animals. Suddenly, they speed off to the sides very fast and dives below. The two boys quickly stand to attention.

                    ANGELINA
              Boys, get back.

                    MARCUS
              What is it?

The colonel is up at the controls and sees Alex at the bottom, walking over to everyone at the back edge of the boat.

                    COLONEL
              Oh, that is too obvious.

Ahead of the boat, is a huge wave rising up along with the boat and everyone in it. High up in the air, the water begins to clear with multiple eyes staring directly into the eyes of the colonel. The boat begins to slide down off the jaws of the creature as it gives off a thunderous roar, sending the everyone backwards to the water.

As the boat rises back up to the surface, everyone gets to their feet and turns back around to the front to see the Magma spider before them. But three times it size from it's first appearance at the zoo. The colonel increases the speed of the boat and turns away, but it isn't enough to out run this giant. Bobby looks in terror.

                    BOBBY
           Did that thing get bigger!?
             I think it got bigger!

                    ALEX
           Bobby, get to the cabin!

MARCUS
M.J., go with him!

The spider is moving its massive legs and follows around trying to catch its watery meal. Alex goes over to the cargo welded to the sides of the boat and pops the locks.

MARCUS
We're going to need something more than these pistols of ours.

Alex reveals machine guns and a cannon with ammunition.

MARCUS
That'll do.

Everyone arm themselves and aims upwards. The colonel activates the rail guns on the sides of the boat and fires at the spider's legs, hoping that he can create a gap to escape through. Everyone begin firing as the two boys are watching from the safety of the cabin. Marcus picks up a cannon with 5 nozzles and an inferred scope. The targeting system of the cannon locks onto the belly of the beast.

Five lights leave the cannon. Two lands on the spider's legs and three on the belly.

The belly explodes and Marcus does a fist pump. The explosion also took out one of the spider's legs, allowing the colonel to lead the boat away with the spider following behind. As it follows, one of the spider's legs lands in front of the boat, causing the boat to crash. Sparks is coming out of the panel where the colonel is located and the boat's engine stutters a little. The boat is still maneuvering but not as fast as it was.

Out of the hole of the spider, where the grenades went off, lava is spilling out along with baby spiders. These tiny spiders are crawling over their mother and starts to jump

down. Everyone continues firing as the boat is moving in all
directions

Far above the action about a mile away, an armored chopper
swoops in from the side with soldiers in dark blue suits
scrambling with the sound of the rescue chopper blurring out
the noise of the commotion with the team within. You can hear
panic over the radio as one soldiers is trying to communicate
with the person on the other line.

                        PILOT
              H.Q., this is Transport 9.
            Not getting any response from
            the colonel. But we have spotted
            possible survivors in the ocean.
                What are our orders?

    A response is made over the radio with static. You can hear
the person on the other side, but just bits of words. The
co-pilot adjusts the radio frequency. The operator is coming
in clear now.

                       OPERATOR
            Transport 9, you have the go ahead
            for rescue. The island has already
            been sterilized. Do not, I repeat,
            do not return here. Entire city is
                infected. The plague origin is
            unknown. Head for second base and
                        await . . .

Transmission is cut off.

                      CO-PILOT
                We've lost them.

                     COMMANDER
            Head for the light in the ocean.
            Whether it's our team or civilians,
                we have to get them out.

    The pilot begins descending downwards. Some of the baby
spiders got on board and everyone is firing everywhere. The
colonel is still up top steering the boat with one hand and
fires his magnum gun with the other. He sees a spider making
its way pass Alex and around towards the front of the boat
where there's a window that leads to the cabin.

    The spider tries to make its way through the window, but
the colonel shoots it down and rolls up his sleeve to activate
a beacon for the satellite. The satellite is repositioning

itself as programmed by the colonel and starts to rev up. As the colonel is pushing buttons on the screen of the watch, a baby spider creeps up from the side and lunges at him.

The colonel struggles with the spider and the armband is ripped off his wrist and falls at the bottom next to the window of the small cabin. Bobby takes notice of the device. The colonel kicks the spider back and shoots it overboard. Now another baby spider appears to attack him.

Back at the cabin, Bobby pries open the window and climbs out to grab the colonel's armband while there's firing going around. The colonel sees Bobby picking it up.

                         COLONEL
                 PUSH THE BUTTON, KID!

    Alex turns around. Bobby taps the red activation button on the touch screen of the watch. Angelina twists a high explosive grenade, straps it to a metal canister marked explosive and tosses it upwards to the jaw of the spider. It explodes and the spider rises up in pain. The clouds begin to light up green. As the magma spider is up on its back 4 legs roaring, the colonel pushes forward the throttle and speeds away as a beam of green light hits its target. The Magma spider expands and explodes into a fireball of lava. The wave from the explosion causes the boat to spin out of control and everyone hangs on for dear life.

After everything calmed down, the sound of an engine is heard. Alex looks up to see Transport 9 descending down onto them.

                        COMMANDER
               This is IPA. If there's any
             survivors, please show yourself.

The colonel's hand appears over the steering wheel and rises up. Alex gets up off the floor and to his feet and makes his way over to his brother who is sitting up against a crate.

                        ALEX
               Bobby. You tough
               little soldier.

                        BOBBY
               What a ride.

Alex has a cloth and puts it over Bobby's head. Alex turns
to look over his left shoulder and sees Marcus and his family
hugging each other.

                        BOBBY
               I'm glade it's over.

Alex turns back to his brother.

                        ALEX
                   Yeah.
               It's over . . .
                   for now.

A low beam of light is cast onto the boat as the chopper
is getting into position to lift the survivors out of the
water. The scene changes to the inside of an elevator in
motion with a man wearing civilian clothing and talking on
an earpiece.

                        NEWTON
               Yes, sir. Sorry for the delayed
               transmission. I was on my way to
               retrieve the data as you requested,
               but I encountered a bit of a problem.
               It seems that the agency was tipped off
               of our little experiment and had team sent in.

Newton stops speaking as he listens to the person on the
other side.

NEWTON
Don't worry. The team from the agency
had no idea who I really was. I made sure
they didn't get too close to the truth.

A beeping sound comes from Newton's pocket. He pulls out a
device with a pulsing light.

                         NEWTON
         Yes, I used the nan-nites to lure the
           corpses to the second team that was
          sent in. Unfortunately, they were able
            to escape with survivors. I don't know
          why you had me disable the self-destruct
           sequence. I could of taken care of them.

Newton stops again to listen to the other person on the
line.

                         NEWTON
                       Understood.

The elevator slows down and stops. The doors open to the
outside with trees and grass burnt to a crisp. As if all organic
matter was burned away. There are two fully armed helicopters
waiting with their engines on. A couple of soldiers in red are
carrying the soldier in blue that was at the lighthouse with
bone sticking from it and loading it onto a helicopter in a
cryo-tube.

                         NEWTON
             If it means anything to you,
             I do have a bit of good news.

The back door of the transport carrying the soldier in blue
closes.

                         NEWTON
           Along with the battle data from the
            team you sent in for me, there is a
           specimen on its way to you. They will
            begin experimentation with Professor
              Grounds' bio-nites immediately.

The voice on the other side continues.

                          NEWTON
              The data from Professor Grounds?

     Newton looks up to see Leader with the disk he swiped from
Alex.

                          NEWTON
              I guarantee you the information
                   is back in our hands.

     Newton takes the disk and gets into the second chopper with
Leader following from behind and hops in.

                          NEWTON
              The agency won't know
                   what hit them.

Leader slides the door shut.

1866

"Morning, Mr. and Mrs. Filton. w." Four little boys stands there with smiles on their faces. Mr. Filton comes around the house. "As a matter of fact we do. You can start with the leaves and sticks." "Right away, Mr. Felton." The four boys hurry to work. After Mr. and Mrs. Filton retreats back into their home, John makes a comment on how he's glad for Mr. and Mrs. Filton going back inside.

"You're not still afraid of those rumors are you?" "Yes I'm still afraid. When you have trouble sleeping at night from time to time about kids being taken away by goblins with red eyes, you tend to worry." "If you're so afraid, why do you still work here?" "My dad says that if I quit this job, that he'll put me to work with the other grownups." Fenton rushes over towards them with a bag of trash. "Quick guys, get back to work. Mr. Filton is coming."

"How's it coming" "Good!" "Well, if you boys need anything just give a yell." "Yes, Mr. Filton." Hours pass and the boys begin putting back the tools in the shed. As they were walking back home, Doug trips over a huge chunk of metal and scrapes his knee. "You OK?" "Yeah it's just a scratch. I'll be fine." "I'm going to cut through this path since my home is near by. I'll see you both tomorrow." John departs with his brother Brady from the group as Fenton and Doug continues on.

Arriving at his home, Fenton realizes that his lucky charm was missing. "Are you sure you brought it with you?" "I take it with me where ever I go." "Maybe you dropped it back at the Filtons." "I'll just have to go see." "Do you want me to come with you?" "No. I can go alone. Besides, your dad's waiting for you to do some of your own yard work." "Alright, see you tomorrow." Half way back to the Filtons, Fenton is searching around the ground for his pendant. "Hello there!" Fenton quickly jumps to his feet by the voice of Mr. Filton. "Woe, take it easy young man."

"Mr. Filton, what are doing here?" "I'm just looking for my dog. He appeared to have run off again." "I never knew that you had a dog." "We like to keep to ourselves. Would you like to help me look for him?" "No I can't. I'm trying to find my lucky charm. I've been looking for it." "I could use some luck finding my dog. Sure you don't want to help?" "I really can't." "OK. See you some other time than." A couple of minutes pass and Mr. Filton's dog arrives by his side.

"I was afraid you got hurt. Come on. We got to get dinner back to the misses. But first, we must earn our meal." Mr. Filton holds his balled up hand to his dog's nose and the dog starts to sniff. It growls as it runs off into the forest. "Good boy." With tears going down his cheeks, Fenton decides to give up continue on home with hopes that going back to the Filtons the next day, he'll find his lucky charm laying around in their yard.

Rustling makes its way through the bushes to his far left. Something is there and it is not alone. The sounds stops, and with the sound of a twig snap, Fenton jets off home with a low grunting sound following behind. No matter how fast he keeps running, the sound keeps up with him on both sides now until the sound on his right goes quite followed by the sound on his left. Fenton ducks down behind a tree that had fallen to the ground from the wind storm a couple of days ago.

Something begins tapping Fenton on top of his head. He reaches to feel something wet touching him. It was some sort of slim starting to poor from above. Quickly looking upwards, a grotesque looking animal is staring down at him with giant fangs. Fenton gets to his feet and starts running with the creature hot on his trail. "HELP! HELP!" The four-legged beast isn't the only thing in the woods with Fenton. Fenton looks to his side as he's running and sees something much bigger skipping along with ease just before it disappears.

Nothing ahead but more trees, he looks behind him to see the creature had stopped in its tracks. Fenton turns his head forward just as he comes to a sudden stop. He begins gasping for air and slowly falls to the ground. As he falls, there is an ogre-like creature with red eyes staring down at Fenton. The monster grabs Fenton by the ankles and drags him away with the smaller creature following behind. Fenton is not dead. Eyes wide open with a frozen look, he is unable to move. Only to see in the distance his family's farm getting farther away.

Days have passed and fliers are being put up everywhere about the disappearance Fenton Lone. His friends and family are going around asking everyone about any information on the little boy. Back at the filton's farm, we have Doug, Brady, and John raking up leaves and collecting twigs in silence. Just not saying one word. The front door opens with Mrs. Filton bringing out a tray holding glasses of lemonade in her hand. "I thought you boys could use some refreshments." "Thank you," they replied. "Don't worry. I'm sure he'll turn up somewhere."

A dog appears from out of the bushes with Mr. Filton. Doug takes notice. "Hey, when did you get a dog?" "Oh, pooch. We've had him long before you were born. Say Brady, that is a very nice ring you got there. You're the runner of the group aren't you?" "Yes ma'am. I run all over the place." "Running is a good thing. Promise me you'll never stop running."

THE TRAVELER

THE TRAVELER

A female police officer is standing in a living room covered in dust and sees an old tape recorder lying on the floor. The officer picks it up. With a whisper, "Brand new?" The play button is clicked, followed by a man's voice.

"March 17, 2235. This is my 16th attempt to find the cure to my, little problem. I thought if I went back to where it all began, I could find clues to how I stumbled onto the success of my invention."

The officer continues to listen to the voice on the recorder as she shuffles through old newspapers, with pages practically crumbling in her hands. A piece of the paper that didn't crumble into pieces was partially readable.

"Boy genius wins 1st place at high school science fair with molecule manipulator." The date on the newspaper reads June 2, 2055.
The voice of the man continues.

"I can feel the change inside of me increasing with every jump. I came here to see what I've done that made this possible. Instead I come to a place I barely recognize." The sound of someone sitting on a thick leathery fabric is heard with the sound of the man exhaling as if he's been walking for days. "I never got to see them. Maybe that should be a good thing." He can be heard licking his lips followed by a short-lived laugh.

"It's funny. I should be celebrating my 12th birthday by now. Never even made it to my senior prom. Too young to of been asked, and now too old to ask someone for that matter. Ah! The pain is getting worse. I think, maybe, my last jump should be for a place that makes more sense."

Clicking is now heard over the recorder, followed by a high pitch noise and the sound of the recorder hitting the floor. The officer slowly turns around towards the large window facing the furniture as the light from the sun tries to make its way through the dust covered window, casting shadows on the walls.

Walking away, the officer notices something strange. Her shadow didn't move off an old sofa. The officer walks over to the dusty couch and rubs her finger along the dark image sitting in front of her.

"Ash?" The officer gets on her radio. "Lt." "Go ahead," replies a voice. "Sir, I think you should meet me in the living room." Not a minute later, you can hear footsteps coming down the rotting stairs. "What did you find, Anderson?"

She answers with ash falling off her hands. "I found the same type of ash we got locked up in evidence from old case files. Spread out in the form of a person. This can't be a coincidence. Very strange."

The Lt. hands Anderson a photo album with photos and papers inside. "What's this?" "Something I found in a wall safe upstairs. There's a letter inside. More like suicide letter." "What do you mean?"

"It seems that one Melissa Talpert gave up her son for adoption and instructed the agency never to reveal what happened to his parents." Melissa Talpert? I know that name." "The mother of one Danny Talpert. The boy genius."

"Of course, my grandfather went to school with him, and went on and on how this kid made a cat go from one box to another at the end of the cafeteria with light at his high school science fair."

"As you told me over and over again after I took you on as my partner." Anderson stands up and looks over to the Lt. "What I didn't tell you was that Danny did find out about his father's death and his mother's suicide and became very disconnected from society."

She walks back over to the dusty window. "He then went missing a year later. Never heard of again. But not before spending weeks on end at his mother and father's grave." Static comes over both of their radios, followed by a voice.

"Unit 13, we have a report of a possible grave robbery in the Stretson Cemetery. Get this, a witness says that he saw a man walk out of a light in the middle of the graveyard."

The Lt. responds on his radio with a grin. "We're on our way. Lets go officer. We'll leave this place to forensic." Anderson lays the photo album on an old desk next to a busted flowerpot and leaves with her partner.

THE RUNNERS

THE RUNNERS

Scene opens at ground level, panning along quickly with a man wearing worn down high priced shoes and business suit with sweat stains all over. Behind this man comes another man wearing shorts and muscle shirt. Another person follows, and many more, nearly out of breath and running for their lives.

High above is a helicopter from channel 12 news continuing its coverage on the situation. "We are back at the scene of an astonishing event. Hundreds of people all over America are making their way here in Roswell. The local authorities are still following behind, but not taking any action."

Inside of one of the police cars, the officer in the passenger seat just gets off the radio and tells the driver to start slowing down to a stop. "Finally the military is taking charge." The cars all comes to a stop as hundreds of people continue running towards a blockade constructed by the U.S. Army armed with guns and a few with mega-phones connected to speakers.

Back at news 12 station people are moving fast throughout the rooms and on the set with files in hand and talking with other reporters on cell phones. Coverage is being held at multiple airports, road checkpoints, and hospitals as thousands of more people are running the streets, trying to head west like a flock of birds during migration.

A woman in a suit is walking quickly with a folder at hand while talking on a cell phone. "What are you saying?" The scene changes to a man on a balcony of a hotel. "I'm saying the event happening in the states is happening here." We leave this man and journey across the streets of London filled with runners, and now along open fields of grass.

These runners of England aren't running to Mexico, but to Stonehenge, as if they were being summoned. Just like Americans to Roswell, and everyone else around the world. All heading towards historic landmarks of their homeland. Back at the news 12 station, they are on the air feeding the viewers live coverage of this historic event with a man sitting on a bench in the waiting area of a hospital mumbling to himself, until a little girl comes wondering along and sits beside him with a smile. "My mommy's here for a check up. Not me. I don't get sick." "That's a good thing. I can't remember the last time I got sick myself." On the TV, a reporter is making another announcement.

"We are now getting conflicting reports that the military is giving the go ahead to shoot on site if these citizens can't be stopped. Back on the scene where military is being told to stand down for fear of a mass slaughter, jeeps and barricades are being moved. "This will be the day our secret got out." The commander turns with a worried look. "They're too busy running towards something to care what we're hiding, son." Runners all over the world are running pass the blockades and military forces. Even though many forces around the world are sticking by their policies and begin opening fire, others are witnessing history in the making, not knowing why thousands are running towards Earth's famous landmarks.

Suddenly one by one, runners are disappearing all over the world. "Oh my . . . I . . . I can't believe this," screams a reporter. "They're disappearing." An anchorman comes on to report to everyone watching and listening to the radios about the disappearance of thousands of people all over the world with out explanation. That's when volcanoes begin erupting, spewing ash to the sky, causing serious ripple effect with nature. It's as if someone took ahold of the planet and shook it. Buildings falls, oceans rise high and covers cities like a blanket. Panic is in the streets and back at the hospital, a mother is screaming for her daughter who was talking to the mysterious man. "Gloria! Gloria, where are you?" Gloria and the man was nowhere to be found as the mother is trampled. People on the streets are running pass TV displays in store windows and on the TVs we see the space station falling to earth and a huge explosion in the sky. The sun disappears for a few seconds, causing darkness everywhere. Then it reappears as a different color, sending an energy wave forward, shattering the planet into pieces along with the moon and the inhabitants along with the other planets in the solar system.

Ships launched from the moon were affected by the super nova and their electronics went dead, leaving them floating helplessly in space, back towards earth's locations now occupied by a newly formed hole in space.

GHOSTS

GHOSTS

We see a broken-up driveway, on a fall night with leaves blowing pass the dead trees and rotting bushes. Through the fog we see headlights, and behind these headlights is a rusty old van. The van drives across the broken up driveway and parks in front of a very old 3 floor mansion with many broken windows.

The van's engine followed by the headlights are turned off. The van doors open and out comes two men in their early 20's with small pieces of equipment around their necks and shoulders. Kyle look upon this abandoned home while Rick is opening the back doors of the van to grab more stuff. "Hey, you want to give me a hand?" "Rick, I can't believe you took a call, knowing that we're on our way to meet Elizabeth at the airport."

"Don't worry. This place has been here for years and not one mention of any activity. It'll be a quick and easy job and some extra cash in our pockets. We'll meet up with your girlfriend with time to spare. Then spring break can begin." The two brothers gather up their stuff and begins heading towards the front door of the mansion.

As the front door opens, we hear a creaking sound. "Rick, how many times will you be making that sound when we go into an old building?' "Ah, c'mon. Every place we've been to, the doors don't creek. Don't you find that weird?" Kyle turns to his brother with a frown. "I find it weird that you kept track of all the doors we've passed through."

The two brothers are now in the main room with spiders moving along their webs containing dead bugs, rodents running along the wooden floor, and a giant chandelier slowly twirling back and forth. Rick shines his flashlight upward. "Hey, Kyle." "What?" "No dust on the chandelier." "Hey, Rick." "What?" "I don't care." Kyle continues to put up little sensors.

"You're not even looking." "That's because I'm trying to set this stuff up. You going to help me or not?" As soon Rick takes the light off of the chandelier, dozens of eyes are shown, looking down below onto our two ghost hunters. Equipment was set up in the main room. Kyle pushes a button to activate everything and tosses a bag to Rick. "Lets get this over with." They go through out the rooms placing tiny blue sensors for the camera in the main room to see, beginning with the kitchen.

Rick sees the ceiling fan as a good place to put the sensor. He climbs up onto the unstable kitchen table while Kyle watches closely. The table is creaking with dust falling off. The sensor is placed and the table gives away, sending Rick falling backwards into Kyle's arms. "My hero." Kyle drops his brother to the floor and continues onto the next room. "We'll get through this place faster if we separate." The kitchen door closes. The scene changes to the third floor of the home, the kids bedroom where the ghost was reportedly scene. Rick places a sensor on the window and immediately picks up something on his PDA.

"Kyle?" "Go ahead." "I'm picking up multiple signals in the basement. Very weak, with one giving off normal readings. Is that you?" The scene changes to the basement with Kyle standing near dozens of bodies. "Yep, and I'm not alone. You better get down here." "On my way." While Rick is making his way to the lower level of the house, Kyle is examining everyone he sees. He comes to an old man and his eyes widen with a bit of a fear look on his face. "Rick, you need to get down here right now. We've got bodies everywhere. One of them is Mr. Goldman." "I'll be right there." Kyle picks up a journal near the feet of his historian professor who went missing 2 weeks before the semester ended.

Kyle picks up the journal and reads the last entry. "I've entered a secret room. Must be the basement. I can't believe it. Bodies everywhere. Some of them are recognizable to me. The batteries in my devices must be dying out. The current in the atmosphere could be draining them. Not that I should trust them anyway. I believe the voices I've been hearing, along with ghostly shadows, and false signals on my device are the spirits leading me to something. Their intensions is yet unknown to me." As Kyle is spending time reading the journal, Rick is stopped coming down the stairs of the second floor by another entity.

He pulls out his homemade camera-gun and flashes at the entity, but misses. "You're not getting away that easily, 29." The ghost toys with Rick with a cat and mouse game until Rick finds himself all turned around, not knowing where to go. He then pulls out his radio. "Kyle?" "Hey where are you?" The scene changes back to the basement and as we can still hear the two brothers continues to communicate, we see the body of Rick lying by the basement door lifeless along with his brother, who is lying by the feet of his college professor.

Strangely, the brothers can still be heard speaking to one another on their walkies. "Rick, what's taking you so long?" "I'm running into heavy activity here. You should get up her." "Sure thing. Where are you?" "Can't say. We'll just have to find each other." Something grabs Rick's ankle pants and drags him away as the basement door closes.

Outside of the mansion is a car pulling up with a woman and a ten year old girl stepping out with flowers at hand. The flowers are laid down where the van once was parked. "Be safe, Kyle." "Love you, daddy."

1947

1947

A family living up on top of a hill are getting ready for their morning chores. "If you two boys don't get down here right now, you'll do double the work with no meals!" Be right down, dad." As the two brothers rush down stairs, Ruth is in the kitchen with her Elizabeth preparing breakfast. "Took you two long enough. Now hurry up before your food gets cold." Soon after the food was cleaned off the plates, John took his two boys Tom and James outside to start their chores. Hours pass during the hot sun. "Alright boys, go ahead and take a break before lunch."

James decides to take a quick break with his articles as his brother is picking up sticks to play catch with the family dogs, wolf and nightshade. "Always with your nose in the articles. Why don't you ever like to play like other kids?" "This is much more fun than tossing sticks." "I can't believe that Mr. Eckleson lets you take those out of the library." "It's a library. You can take stuff as long as you return them." Tom picks up some of the articles and looks them over with an unimpressed expression on his face.

"I don't see what the big deal is. I've seen short stories longer than what you're reading." "They're snippets of our history, or future. How cool it would be to travel in time." "Well we're in the here and now, and I say now we play, not read. Come on, lets teach these two how to fetch." "What for? Those two are the dumbest dogs alive." "No they're not. I'll show you." They both start playing with the dogs by tossing sticks back and forth. While being distracted by fighting over one stick, the dogs didn't notice the second one being tossed overhead. As Tom is wrestling with the dogs over the stick, James runs off to retrieve the second one that landed near a tree.

After picking it up and begins walking away, James hears whispering from behind. "Who is it? Who's there?" He slowly walks forward and towards the voices and finds that the sounds are coming from a tree. Out of curiosity, James begins rubbing the tree with his hands. Then suddenly, a force pulls his arm within, trying to absorb his body. Hearing the fainted scream, the two dogs runs to the direction of the tree with Tom not far behind. Tom jumps and grabs James' legs and pulls as hard as he could until James was set free.

"James, you OK?" "Yeah. I'm fine." Once Tom got his brother to his feet, they'd hurried back to the house to tell what had happened. "A tree tried to eat you. I think you two have been out in the sun too long." "Were not imagining any of this, dad. It really happened." "Well, lets ask you two witnesses, OK? Wolf, Nightshade, have you two seen any monster trees coming from the woods?" "Now John, quit making fun," interrupts Ruth. Will you please take the boys to the tree to see what's the fuss is all about?" The father huffs and grabs his coat. "Ok, lets go you two."

Arriving at the site, John picks up a stick and starts to poke the tree all over. "There doesn't seem to be any monster trying to pull me in." "But it did happen. If it wasn't for Tom, I would have been pulled in all the way." "Nothing seems to be happening now, so lets not worry about it. Come on, lunch should be ready and we have much more work to do." The three of them walks away not only leaving behind the so-called man eating tree, but something metal laying beside it. It's an arm made of heavy metal with what appeared to be wearing a white torn fabric, human skin hanging off of it, and a red light pulsing slowly on its wrist. The arm twitches a little and pulse slows down until it pulses no more.

As the day ends and night begins, everyone gets cleaned up and heads off to bed. Later that night, Tom wakes up from a noise. "James, what is it?" "Shhh. Quiet. You're going to wake up mom and dad." "What are you doing?" "Dad may not believe us, but I know what I saw. So I'm going back to that tree." "No you're not." The sound of the window is heard opening. Tom gets to his feet to follow his silly little brother. They both arrive back at the spot where the tree stands, but the tree wasn't there anymore. "James, where is it?" "It just disappeared." "What do you think happened?" "I'm not sure. I don't think we should stay to find out."

Being cold and frightened, they both ran back home to find a stranger in a white long jacket with a symbol of the American flag on his right arm, standing in the front room. Because of the commotion, Ruth and John ran down stairs to see what was going on. "Will you please tell your old man just what is going on?" Everyone sees this man in a long white jacket and scratches on his face as if he was in a fight, speaking to them without sound. John demands answers and starts to get frustrated. As John approaches the man in white, a vortex appears with another figure appearing from behind, trying to make its way through.

The blast blows everyone to the floor, sucking the two mysterious figures back in, leaving the family lying on the floor in a dazed state. The mother looks over to her daughter, very good at reading what people are saying from a long distance, mouthing what the man in white was saying. "Honey? Honey, what is it?" "Don't go . . . Don't go . . ." "Don't go where?" "What is a Sirius B?"

THE DARK
WITCH

THE DARK WITCH

A tired horse slowly makes its way to the kingdom of Nom and on this tired steed is an equally tired warrior. Both dirty, scarred, covered in blood and ready for a good meal and a good night sleep. A horn is blown and the gates open. After entering, the warrior hops down with his bloody bag of troll hearts.

"Can we get you anything, sir?" "Let the cook know I'm in dire need of a good meal." "Of course. Anything else?" The warrior's horse falls over and doesn't move. "I'll need a new horse." The scene changes to a room full of potions, sacred scrolls spread everywhere, and an old man with a long beard and pointy hat mixing a blend of powder and liquids in a giant pot.

"I have to say, wizard, this isn't your type of magic." "Sometimes desperate times calls for desperate measures," says a woman in red. "WITCH!" "Duncan, no!" The wizard gets between the warrior and the witch. "What do you mean no? She's the reason why Eldredge fell. Why my family is dead." "As much as I like to take credit for such a thing, the reason for the slaughter lies elsewhere." "Duncan, the phantom dragon will not be your target. It's not feeding on the children of the land, but collecting their energy for something."

"What are you saying, wizard?" "He speaks the truth. I'm the last of the witches. The others are dead, along with the wizard council. The only way to defeat the dragon is to destroy its creator. A witch once thought to be dead for years have returned to finish what she had started. This witch is more evil than the rest of us. A darker witch." You and your kind aren't exactly fairy godmothers." The witch frowns. "Do you have the hearts?" Duncan holds tightly his bag. "Go ahead and give it to her. I have something to show you." He gives the hearts to the witch and follows the wizard while she mixes the ingredients. "Here you go. An axe forged on Mount Orone by the council themselves, an amulet that harnesses ones inner strength, and finally, Dobber." "What's a Dobber?" An eagle appears from behind and lands on Duncan's shoulders.

"Your guide to the source of evil. Now you must rest, for if you fail, the lands will be ruled in fear forever." "I will leave at first light." "Where you're going, there will be no light." The night passes and Duncan is on a new horse. The eagle flies high with Duncan and a group of knights making their way towards the mountains, knowing that this journey will not be an easy one. As time goes by, this band of warriors gets smaller and smaller until their was just Duncan on his horse. This source of evil must of known of their campaign against it, for the challenges was more than he expected.

Lost and hungry, he looks up to see the eagle land on a tree, leaning to the side as if it was trying to show him something. He rides up to the tree to see nothing but fog. "What now?" The ground begins to rumble and out of the fog leaps a griffin of enormous size. It roars and charges at him. The eagle swoops down to gouge out one of the griffin's eyes. The griffin roars and eagle swoops down for another attack. "Crazy bird." The bird surprises the warrior by increasing its size to match the griffin. He dodges out of the way while these two goliaths battles it out.

"Duncan," whispers a voice. He turns. "Come to me, Duncan." Duncan picks up his axe and follows the soft voice to a bridge that leads to a castle. With the light from the amulet, Duncan was able to make his way to a chamber with the stench of hate in the air. "Duncan." "Show yourself." Part of the concrete floor begins to move to the center of the room to form a person with long hair, wearing a gown and a staff at hand. Our warrior is startled to what he sees. "I see you remember me." "Mother?"

She pulls him towards her and forces him to look at the ceiling. The image displayed shows the dragon trying to break its way through the wizard's shield around Nom. "Soon as my child breaks through, I will be unbeatable." Duncan blinds her with the light from the amulet and she zaps him through the wall. She then gains power from the dead to feed her creation more power. The shield is broken, leaving Nom unprotected. Duncan comes to and sees his wife and child standing next to him. "We love you so much. We know you can do it."

The amulet begins to glow stronger and back to his feet he goes. A beam of yellow light comes through the wall towards the witch, but she stops it with a red light coming from her staff before she hits the wall. Duncan walks through with the amulet around his neck and the axe in his hand. "Child, you were my greatest mistake. A mistake I'll gladly erase from the Earth." She fires a red beam as he fires a yellow light. On the ceiling, the wizard and witch's beam of power is holding off the dragon's flames.

"This world is mine, warrior." Duncan gives everything he had through the axe. Both of them cause an explosion throughout the dark castle and over the dark land. The dragon inhales and launches a huge fireball, but nothing happens as the flame disappears before impact. The people of Nom begin cheering as loud as they could. "He did it," says the witch. "Yes he did," replies the wizard. Back at the Dark Castle, in the middle of the destroyed chamber, stands the dark witch and Duncan pointing their weapons at each other, frozen in stone.

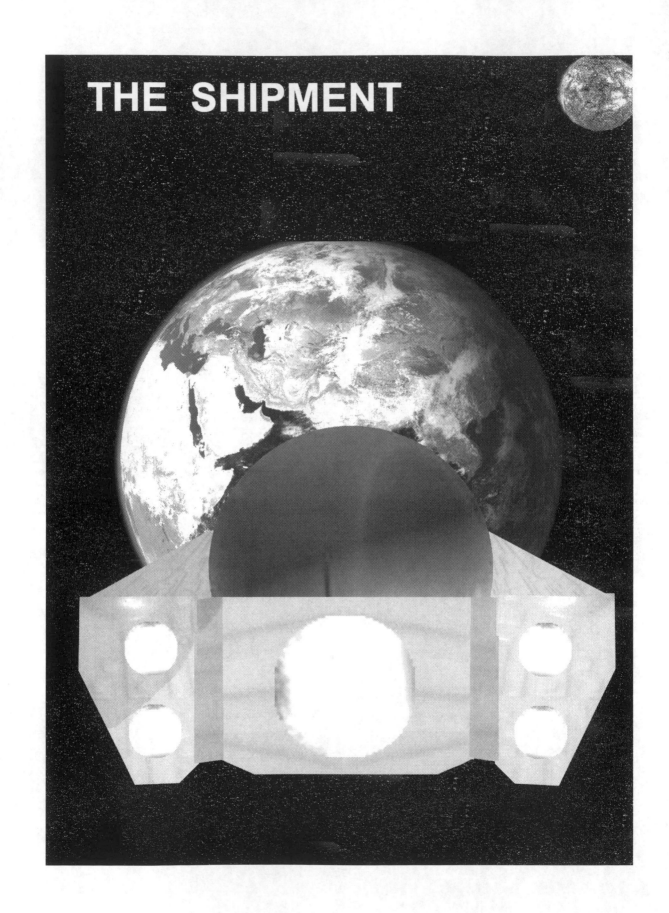

THE SHIPMENT

Entering into a room full of computer monitors and blinking lights, we hear the sounds of clicking and beeping. In front of a large monitor is a chair, and in the chair is a man in a blue one piece uniform with captain Ethan Chan on his collar.

A faint alarm goes off, grabbing his attention and making him spill a blue liquid out of his cup and onto his shirt. Ethan grabs a clipboard, and walks to the elevator to make his way down to the lower deck.

The scene changes to a massive room that has huge steal pipes going from the ceiling to the floor, creating a long corridor with more pipes and gages along the way. An elevator door opens. Ethan walks out and heads straight for a small 2-door jeep with a picture of Earth on the side.

Ethan is driving through this area while whistling a tune as he's scanning giant bar codes next to the pipes with gages. "Looking good. Looking good." He turns a corner and passes statues of what looks to be people of great importance, greeting them as if they were going to respond. "Hello. Calling it a night? Just to let you know, traffic is a bit hectic." He's just smiles away as he continues driving pass more statues.

Ethan finally arrives to a huge door, 20ft high with statues of armed soldiers equally tall on both sides. "Good evening. I'm just here for some maintenance before calling it a night. What, no response?" He leans over to a panel and puts his left eye to it. A green light flickers as the machine scans his retina.

The 20ft high doors slowly opens up and Ethan drives on through. "Gentlemen." Entering a huge dome area with sealed doors all over the walls. He parks the jeep and gets out to make his way to a chair in the middle of the room. No computer monitors or wires, just a simple looking steel chair with a small metal rod protruding out of its left arm.

Ethan is walking along, still whistling his toon, and gets up to the chair, ready for his maintenance check. A circular scar can be seen after he rolls up his sleeve. He then aligns the circular scar to the metal rod and pushes down. "Hello, computer." With his eyes closed, a voice of the ship's computer is over heard as we enter through the captain's forehead with wires and rotating parts lighting up with electricity.

The computer continues to speak to the captain as he continues to sit in the chair. "Executing level-3 maintenance. Charging time, 2 hours and 45 minutes." "Computer, any mail?" The computer goes silent for a few seconds. "You have 13 messages."

"Any from my wife?" "You have 1 message from Evelyn. Would you like to hear it first?" "Yes, please do." The computer starts the audio file immediately.

"Hi, honey. I just want to start off and say that I love and miss you very much. Everything is looking well with the cryo-tube and you seem to be holding up very well. You should be back to normal as soon as the rest of us meet up with you. I had to pull your son away from the window as everything was breaking up. It's a bit unsettling. It's beautiful and sad at the same time. To know that you really can't go home again."

The computer stops the audio file. "We have arrived at Orbagron site. We'll be landing in 7 minutes." "Alright, continue playing back messages and release cargo starting with the herbivores." "Complying with directive order 39972. Earth 5 habitation underway."

"Wake me when it's done." The scene changes to a planet full of trees and other vegetation, and through the clouds appears a giant saucer with a dome in the middle. The ship lands and hundreds of cargo doors begins opening. The doors stops halfway and begins closing. "Override sequence initiated."

"Who's overriding?" "The source is coming from outside of the ship." Ethan quickly detaches himself from the chair. Not able to access any of the doors to the bridge, he goes through an emergency hatch.

On top of the ship, a hatch opens and Ethan makes his way out to see a group of armed soldiers with the same logo on their uniforms as he has on his. Ethan just stares at them as one holds up a device and activates it. He falls to his knees and everyone begins heading towards the ship. The man with the device gets on his radio.

"Command, you won't believe this. The cargo we lost, has arrived. You might want to alert the president that her great . . . great . . . great . . . grandfather is here to see her."

THE DINNER

We see a man eating a cheeseburger with one hand and driving with the other. He passes an old bus stop belonging to a school that was shut down. The town folk keep it up in memory of Anna Marie Jenkins. An hour later, Brett sees a diner and pulls over to use the rest room.

As he pulls up to park, the lights of the diner goes out except for a couple of florescent bulbs flickering on and off. Brett goes up to the door and begins knocking on the glass. "Hello?" Looking through the window, he gets a view of someone walking into the kitchen. It looks like a little girl. "Hey! Hello!" As he pounds on the door, not getting a response, he turns away and heads back to his car. A door behind him opens up with someone shouting to him.

"Hey, you want in?" Brett looks at the woman behind him and begins walking back to the dinner. "Thanks. I just needed to use the restroom. After drying his hands, Brett tosses the paper towel into the wastebasket, not noticing the front page of a newspaper also in the wastebasket mentioning a car accident taking the life of a little girl.

As he exits the bathroom, the swinging door closes behind. It swings a little back open to reveal to us a clean bathroom, but then swings back open to reveal to us a dingy crud infested atmosphere. "That is one fine bathroom you got here." The waitress looks up to him with a grin. "Well a customer coming out of the bathroom feeling happy is a customer willing to cough of some dough. What'll it be?" "A cup of coffee and a grilled cheese."

The waitress walks into the back leaving Brett to chat with the other customers. Looking to his left, Brett sees a much older gentleman working on a sandwich and a cup of coffee. "How's that sandwich doing for you?" The old man doesn't respond and keeps on nibbling away. "OK, not a talker." Brett turns to another man with a thick beard and a plaid shirt with pants to match. "OK, a plaid lover." Brett just smiles at the man in the dirty plaid hat.

Brett's grin goes away as he's being looked down by brown eyes, dark enough to be pure black. These eyes are attached to a wrinkly face and some type of black shadowy paste around the eyes. "OK, gothic plaid lover." Brett turns to the sound of a spoon tapping a plate. It was a man wearing a gas attendant uniform just tapping away on his plate of food crumbs. The clanking stops and the attendant looks up at Brett. "You Brett?" "That's a good guess." "Not a guess. Just a fact." Brett walks over to the table and sits down in front of the man, looking at him with no recollection of them ever meeting.

"I'm sorry, have we met?" "No, but you've met my daughter. Ever since you took here away from me, a gaping hole was left in my chest, until I couldn't stand it any longer. First my wife left me. Now three years later, my little Anna. But that's all in the past now." Brett hears a plate hit the table, grabbing his attention. It's his grill cheese. The waitress leaves the check next to his food and walks back to the kitchen. "What ever, man." He sits down and begins eating, looking at his check, not wanting to touch it like most people.

He hears the sound of giggling and turns to see the girl from earlier sitting across from the man at the table drinking a milk shake. The waitress lays two separate checks for the man and the girl and walks away. As Brett stares at the girl with familiarity, the man at the table stares back at him. The two people sitting on Brett's side moans, grabs their checks, and walks out the door. "I didn't know the food was free. Why bother giving out checks?"

The waitress wipes the counter as if she doesn't hear him. The man and the little girl lay their saucer and cups onto the counter next to Brett and heads towards the door. "Hey, do I know you?" The girl just waves with a smile with her check in her hand. "Sir, you ready to check out?" Brett picks up the check to view his bill. He freezes with images before him. These images are familiar to him. Images of himself playing ball with kids at a birthday party with his name on a cake with 9 lit candles, walking across a stage in front of many people, it's his high school graduation. More images are appearing of what was just a part of his past, including one recent event of him driving along the road, without notice, heading right for a little girl on a bicycle and heading for a bridge. Brett starts to come out of it, coughing up muddy water, trying to get some air in his lungs.

"What was that?" "You know what it was. Question is, what are you going to do now?" Brett turns to the diner door and notices for the first time, writing above. "Portarius." Slowly moving his hand towards the check in fear of going through the experience again, we can hear the waitress chuckling. "Well, it's not going to bite your hand off." Brett picks up the check and slowly turns in his stool. Looking up, he comes to the realization that he was fooling himself, what he had done, and that there was no turning back. He begin heading to the door and turns to see the waitress looking at him. "Who are you?" "Someone just doing her job, Brett." "What will happen to me?" "Good things, sir. Good things." Brett heads out the door and into the thick fog with the door closing behind.

THE SCULPTURE

THE SCULPTURE

Joel Ackerman, the founder of "The Museum of Ancient Arts", is in the loading dock area with an inventory list, preparing for the grand opening. An opening he's been waiting for his whole life. Ever since he was a kid visiting his uncle's museum filled with trophies from his animal safaris from around the world. The bedtime stories of his adventures would always put Joel to sleep. There would be many mornings where he would wake up from dreams of hunting animals, visiting the natives of far away lands, and watching them perform their rituals.

"Joel, everything is set up for the artifacts." "Thanks, Vern. Just leave the keys with the guard on your way out." "Will do." Ten minutes later a man in a jump suit enters with a clipboard of his own. "Sorry for my tardiness. But the artifacts are finally here." "It's about time. What took you so long?" "The team had trouble getting the sculptures away from the tribe. They wouldn't give them up until after their ceremony was complete." "What kind of ceremony?" "Something about the end of the world. Or a start of a new beginning. I can't be sure. We had to watch from a distance and most of our questions were being ignored."

"I'm sure it wasn't all that bad." "Well, the food was good." "I'm just happy your team made it back in time. By the way, where's Kenny?" "He's in the show room getting everything organized." "Alright people, lets get a move on. We have to get this fixed up by tonight for Mr. Ackerman. This is a big night and everything must go perfectly." "I see you have everything under control." "Joel, I was just making sure that everything would be ready for tonight." "Good. The sculptures?" "They're right over there in the crates. Would you like to do the honors?" "Don't mind if I do."

Joel takes the crow bar and forces the lid open. A powerful burst of wind comes rushing out with an awful smell. "What did you guys do to the crate?" "Nothing. It must have been the tribe." "No matter. I just need the smell gone and everything set up before I return this evening." "It'll be done. You can count on us." Ten hours later, Joel returns quickly to his office with files falling from his arms. "You're late." "Ralph, I'm not in the mood. Everything's ready?" "Yes, we're just waiting for your approval." "What about our main guests?" "They should be here anytime."

"Why, here they come now," mentions Theo as he continues to sweep around the cases. All ten representatives arrived in suits with folders in their hands. "Gentleman. The opening will begin shortly. If you would just follow me to my off . . ." "We are eager to view the stone sculptures if you don't mind?" "Of course. Right this way." Ralph quickly pulls out a set of keys and opens the door to the room, where the sculptures are being displayed. He then sets the keys on a cabinet and turns on the display lights, showing a painting of a rain forest and a huge waterfall.

One by one everyone begins to clap together with a smile. One of the businessmen puts his hand on Joel's shoulder and tells him that this opening will be a success. He then walks out of the room with the other associates to gather around a table in the dinning room. As Joel's out giving his speech to the full crowd of people in the showcase room, a janitor enters the display room of the tribal artifacts and begins tying up any loose ends. From a crack in the floor, an ant comes through, crawling all over one of the statues.

Approaching one of the eyes, an electric shock sends the ant to the floor. The faint sound catches the attention of the janitor, who was in the closet at the time putting things away. The janitor slowly walks towards the curtains where the display was hidden. He takes his broom and begins opening the curtains, not only to see a huge hole in the floor, but smashed sculptures lying everywhere. He then turns around from the sounds of objects falling. While he's picking up the pieces, the light goes out and the door slams shut.

"Hey! What's going on? Come on. Quit fooling around. Max? Chester? Anyone?" As he starts walking towards the door to leave, a shelf slams in front of him, blocking his exit. Heavy footsteps circles around him, as if he was being hunted. The lights flicker on and off, casting shadows of a moving object. The janitor begins yelling and swinging the broom in the air like a mad man. An arm swipes him in the back of his leg, knocking him to the floor. He's then grabbed and slung against the wall. The loud noise caught the attention of everyone in the main showroom. Joel heads to the room and starts pounding on the door with Ralph.

"Ralph, where's the keys?" "I must of left them on the table inside the room. I'll go get something to pride the door open." Once the noise stopped, everyone stands quietly and Joel slowly reaches over to the door handle. The door and walls begin to shake all over, followed by a low moaning sound. Ralph returns with two other workers and a crow bar. "On the count of three. 1 . . . 2 . . . 3!" The door is opened and they all stand there shocked by the burn marks all over the walls.

"Joel, take a look at this." Joel walks up to Ralph to see the janitor lying on the floor, burned to a crisp. Along with hundreds of ants crawling all over in and outside of the body.

2024

2024

With a whisper, "Why hello. Pay dirt." Up goes Mile's riffle and aims it straight at the deer. "1...2..." "Hey, Miles!" "Ah!" Miles accidently fires into the air, causing the deer to run off. "Great, Elton. What's the matter with you? You made me give up a perfect kill." "Once you see what we found, you won't care. Come on." Miles and Elton arrive at the hole that the others found. Miles then drops his riffle and runs to the uncovered object with his eyes wide open. "Is it what I think it is?" "That and more." "Find something else, Pearl?" "Something incredible. Everyone, quickly walk this way." After entering, they're all amazed with what they see. "Amazing," whispers Elton. "Is this the only room, Pearl?" "Rick, I couldn't tell you. I've been too busy here in what seems to be the control room."

"Where are you off to now". "I'm going to get my camera." Miles climbs back out of the ship as quickly as he could. Pearl puts down a cube, which causes a view screen to appear. "Hey, Miles! Come and see this." Miles doesn't give a response. Not responding for the third time, Elton decides to go up after him. "Hey guys, you better get up here." As they all exit the craft, they find themselves surrounded by men in black.

Back at the Nevada command center, General Reece was advising the higher-ups about the situation. One of the figures on the screen interrupts the general. "Are the hunters contained?" "Yes, sire. As soon as the craft's sensors were activated, our satellites picked up the transmission, which allowed us to send the closes retrieval team to investigate. The hunters memories are being taken care of as we speak." "Sounds like everything's in order." "Any new details on the fleet?" "Just that the armada has entered our solar system, and that because of the distortion, we can't be sure when they'll enter Earth's orbit."

A nock on the door is heard. "Gentlemen." The general turns off the monitor. "Enter." "Sir, our men are at the airport awaiting the arrival of the professor." "Make sure his equipment is set up exactly as he instructed." "Yes, sir." "Also have him meet me and the others in the conference room soon as he arrives." "Yes, sir." After the sergeant leaves, the general begins collecting up folders and leaves through the other door.

At the airport are two secret agents on stand by for the professor's arrival. As they wait, other service men are keeping in contact with one another to make sure everything's clear. "What's taking so long?" "Patients. He'll be here. That's his plane right now. 3 and 4, how's the view?" "Clear from our spot. He's heading your way." "Copy that. As soon as he enters the building, head on back to base. Stevens and I will take care of it from here." Just when the professor walked through the door, Stevens and Class approaches him right away.

"Professor Nabel? I'm agent Class and this is agent Stevens." "Did my equipment arrive promptly?" "Yes. Your instructions have been followed to the letter and prime candidates have been selected for the travel. But we must hurry." "Understood." Once Nabel and the two agents arrive at an underground passageway, Class waits for an entrance that leads to a lower level and off they go to a door with a man standing by. "Please step out of the car." Seven more guards appear from the dark corners, holding up weapons. Class gets out with Nabel, leaving Stevens in the car. "This is our stop, professor. Good luck to you." "Good luck to us all."

HOURS PASS . . .

An MP puts in a code on a panel, quickly opens the door and sees Nabel at a computer next to a chalkboard full of equations. "Sir, we have to go." "One more second." The room and hallways begins shaking with the ceiling falling apart. "Sir, now!" "Alright, lets go!" Nabel grabs his white coat and is lead through the hallways passing gunfire as military forces are engaging giant grey mechanical soldiers with glowing red-eyed creatures inside.

Nabel enters a room with a circular panel of light, leaving the MP to defend the room from the outside. Nabel sees a tall man at the control panel. "I see you're getting it up and running." Nabel looks at a monitor to view the human race defending itself against the UFOs. "We have one chance to prevent this from happening." He looks at the codes being punched in by the other scientist. He then notices something not right and tries to move pass to correct the problem. "These numbers don't add up. If you do this, the cannons will spit out energy instead of sucking the invaders energy." The tall man grabs Nabel by the throat and lifts him up off the floor.

As the professor is gasping for air, the tall man pushes a button and the outside cannons shoots out beams to the moon, sending a light back to earth, shutting down earth's defenses one by one. We can hear transmissions from soldiers breaking up over the radio before everything goes silence. Being too far underground and shielded, the room is still active with Nabel struggling with his device at hand. The device makes contact with the tall man's chest and lights up.

The tall man is thrown back into a large power generator by a charge with Nabel getting back to his feet and placing his device into a circular slot to activate the portal. The tall man rips away from the scorched wall, leaving half his face on the melted generator and reveals to us that underneath he was a walking machine. The time portal opens and Nabel makes a run for it with the machine soldier jumping at him from behind. The portal closes, leaving the professor trapped in time and the fate of humanity up in the air.

THE END.